Bunny Foo Foo

BOOK #1

BEWARE THE WHITE RABBIT

E.V. DEAN

For Nuche – forever and always.

FIRST EDITION, April 2025
Copyright © 2025 E.V. Dean

Horror World Books
Los Angeles, California

PROLOGUE

Little Sandy Sommers runs through the tall spring grass as quarters jingle and jangle in the pocket of her overalls. She's on the hunt. Her little arms are full of plastic pastel-colored eggs as she embarks on a race against the clock to collect as many eggs as she can before the other kids in the neighborhood get them.

These eggs aren't filled with candy like some of the other Easter egg hunts she's been to in her short six years of life, though. These ones are full of cold hard cash. Coins—and even a few with dollar bills!

If Sandy can just collect enough eggs, maybe she can go get herself an ice cream from Stillwells. If she has her own money, surely her mother will have to take her, won't she?

As Sandy runs through the grass, she imagines the perfect ice cream: chocolate chip, with rainbow sprinkles, in a chocolate-covered waffle cone. If she finds enough eggs, maybe she can even get herself another scoop of ice cream! If so, she will choose mint chocolate chip. It's her second favorite flavor and her father's favorite.

The field is a large sprawling green between the edge of the football field and the forest. In the small city of Berlin, New Hampshire, the view of the White Mountains towers over the clearing.

It's one of the first days in months that the sun shines so brightly that it's melting the white snow caps on the mountains.

Peeking out through the tall grass, Sandy finds her target. A pink pastel egg nestled in the greenery. She quickly bends down, picks it up and cracks open the plastic egg with her small fingers. Nestled inside is a dollar bill! Yes! Victory.

She smiles from ear to ear and shoves the dollar in the pocket of her overalls as she looks around her. Most of the other children are egg hunting closer to the baseball field, but she can't help but feel that if she keeps inching away, toward the forest, she will find even more money.

Sandy takes a few more steps toward the trees and finds another egg. This one is a bright blue pastel egg and she shakes it violently to hear the jingles and jangles she was hoping for. It must be full of coins! She cracks it open and reveals three gold dollars.

"Yes!"

Taking the coins from out of the egg, she slides them into her pocket. Then, when she looks up again, she notices something most peculiar. A sign that she is on the right track to the jackpot.

On the very edge of the forest, sticking out of the bushes and brush are two big rabbit ears, just peeking out over the leaves. They look like the rabbit ears from when Sandy's mother took her to the mall to meet the Easter Bunny a few weeks ago. The Easter Bunny was so sweet to her, even giving her a chocolate bar while she sat on his lap.

And now—here he was!

Maybe he is hiding in the bushes because he has the egg jackpot, she thinks. *Maybe if I run up to him, he will lead me to even more riches!*

Smiling, she begins to run toward the forest with her blond hair flowing in the wind. She's going to get the best prize—she can feel it with every step of her Converse as she runs through the grass.

But suddenly the bushes rustle and the big rabbit ears go straight back, disappearing into the forest.

Should she follow them?

She runs up to the forest edge and looks into the dark between the trees. She remembers one of the things her mother told her:

Never go into the woods by yourself. Always take a buddy.

Sandy rocks on her heels and stands on her tippy toes as she tries to see where the rabbit went. *Technically* she wouldn't be alone if the rabbit was there too? Even though Sandy is a young girl, she knows that under the rabbit suit is usually an adult or a young person of some sort. Her father told her when

Sandy peppered him with endless questions about the Easter rabbit at the mall and he made it really clear to young Sandy that **the Easter Bunny is NOT real.**

So, if Sandy goes into the woods, she won't *technically* be breaking her mother's rules. She will just be stretching the truth.

Sandy's father also told her: "Sometimes it's better to ask your mother for *forgiveness* instead of *permission*."

Maybe this is one of those times.

· · · · · · ●● **●** ●● · · · · · · · ·

When Sandy walks into the woods the hair on the back of her neck rises. It's cold in the dark. The tall pine trees block out any last bit of light. It looks like it's almost nighttime!

Birds chirp loudly as if they are trying to talk to her. She wonders if maybe they can help her find the rabbit.

The white rabbit.

As she stands in the forest, she remembers a book her father read to her a few weeks ago. It's called *Alice in Wonderland* and a young blond girl follows a white rabbit into the woods. Maybe this is normal. Obviously she's not the first young girl to follow a rabbit. Maybe this is what young girls are *supposed* to do?

Looking around for the rabbit, she doesn't see him. Instead, she sees a path that leads further into the forest. On the path are big rabbit footprints that are bigger than the size of her head! *This must be an awfully big rabbit*, she thinks. *Bigger than the one in Wonderland.*

Next to the rabbit footprints is a line in the dirt, like the rabbit is dragging something along with him.

More prizes! It must be!

Sandy's eyes light up and she decides to walk down the path and further into the woods. As she walks, she puts her feet up against the rabbit footprints. The rabbit's feet must be twice her foot size. Maybe more.

With the thought of prizes comes the thought of the ice cream she'll buy. She can almost taste it on her tongue. Maybe she can even get some hot fudge and whipped cream on top as well?

She begins to walk faster, then breaks into a small jog. The dewy spring air blows through her long golden locks as she runs, excited for the chance to be rich. She can't wait to tell her friend Lily from school what wealth she's garnered. Lily is probably back by the baseball field right now looking for eggs with Gemma. Sandy can't stand Gemma. Gemma is always trying to take Lily away from her.

But when Sandy shows back up at the baseball field with pockets full of riches—surely Lily won't leave her again. In fact, maybe Sandy will have enough money to buy them both a nice ice cream.

Sandy could keep running for days, but eventually the rabbit's footprints stop. It is sudden. Like the rabbit just disappeared into thin air.

So she pauses and looks around her, noticing she is surrounded by tall dark bushes that line the trail.

Confused, she walks over to one of the bushes and puts her little face up to one of the shrubs. Maybe the rabbit went into the thicket! Down a rabbit hole!

Sandy narrows her eyes trying to look closer.

And that's when she sees them.

Two bright yellow eyes that look like severed lemons are staring right back at her on the other side of the bush.

Something is wrong with the eyes, though. Sandy can't quite put her finger on it, but her stomach turns when she sees the big black pupils ogling back at her.

It's just a rabbit.

Nothing more, nothing less.

Or is it a man in a rabbit suit?

Sandy narrows her eyes trying to make out its shape through the thicket. It doesn't look like a suit. It looks like a giant rabbit. Bigger than her dad! And her dad is quite tall.

Just as Sandy decides that it is just a regular old giant rabbit, the creature speaks!

"Hi Sandy!" it says.

The creature smiles showing two big, sharp buck teeth.

Sandy blinks and looks again. Rabbits don't talk—at least the rabbits she's seen. Then again, she's never seen a rabbit this big before.

"Are you the Easter Bunny?" Sandy asks. "Like the real one?"

The creature lets out a low chuckle. "No, Sandy. I'm not the Easter Bunny."

"My dad told me the Easter Bunny isn't real."

The rabbit nods. "Well that's not very nice of him to tell you that! Ruining Easter for a pretty little girl like yourself."

Sandy smiles and sticks her face closer to the thicket. No one has ever called her pretty except her mother.

"Do you want some more Easter eggs, Sandy?" the creature asks. "I have a bunch more on the other side of this brush. I think one of them even has a twenty-dollar bill in it!"

Sandy's eyes widen. The only time she's ever had more than twenty dollars was on her birthday.

"What do you think, Sandy? I can't have all these eggs to myself. Would you like some?"

Sandy nods with enthusiasm. "I sure would!"

"OK, Sandy. Come on through the thicket and I will show you."

Sandy rocks back on her heels … Twenty dollars does sound nice.

"Come on, now Sandy. We haven't got all day. You don't want the other kids to find your spot, do you?"

The rabbit has a point.

Sandy reaches into the bushes to spread away the thicket. When she pushes away the branches, the expression on the rabbit suddenly changes. His smile looks more like a frown. And his big buck teeth are showing like a set of vampire fangs. His long tongue licks his lips.

"I'm not sure about this actually. I want to go ask my mom first," Sandy says as her voice shakes.

Before Sandy can pull away, though, the rabbit extends one of his limbs into the thicket and grabs on to Sandy's little arm. Except his hand isn't a rabbit paw—it looks like a man's hand that is white and furry with long sharp talons.

As the talons pierce her skin, bright red blood spurts into the air. Then he tightens his grip, crunching her bones, and pulls the girl into the thicket.

CHAPTER 1

Berlin Mayor Otto Finch is trying not to take himself too seriously. That being said, this is his first press conference—ever. Even though Otto has been the mayor of Berlin, New Hampshire, for about five years now, nothing really ever happens in this little town in the northeast.

The small city of Berlin is nestled up in the White Mountains, just an hour or so drive from the Canadian border. An old paper mill town, Mayor Finch was doing everything in his power to revitalize this small community that he grew up in. But to be frank—Mr. Finch is a bit of a fish out of water. He's a bit tall—just over six foot three, with chocolate dark skin, and thick black glasses. The Finch family is the only Black family in the little mountain town of Berlin and while Otto spent many of his younger years romping around in Boston, he returned to Berlin to take care of his sweet mother, Bernice, who hasn't left Coos County in over a decade.

"You're going to do great," Bernice says as she straightens out Otto's tie. Bernice is almost a foot shorter than her son now and she reaches up with her arms as Otto bends down to meet her. They stand in the middle of their kitchen—newly renovated—in their little mountain house at the foot of Mt. Cabot. A real estate developer, Otto has an immaculate eye for making the ordinary extraordinary. Otto wasn't immensely wealthy, but he had just enough to build his family the nicest house in Berlin right on the edge of the forest.

"I just can't even believe this is happening," Otto says as his forehead sweats. "Here. In Berlin. I mean sure it happens in big cities. Children go missing. But this is a community! This is our town. Things like this shouldn't happen here."

Otto looks down into his mother's sweet green eyes. It is like taking a sip of whiskey after a long day at work. His mother's presence soothes his soul.

"Things like this happen," Bernice says. "But you are in a good position now to help our community and make them feel safe."

Otto nods fervently. "I will. People deserve answers. They don't deserve for this to be swept under the rug. They deserve accountability for their law enforcement and—"

Before Otto can finish his sentence a little girl with bright red hair enters the room. Her eyes are bloodshot and teary, and she walks with her head hung low into the kitchen.

Bernice lets go of Otto and looks down at young Lily.

"What's going on, little bean?" Bernice says as she bends down to her adopted granddaughter.

Lily sniffles as her pasty freckled cheeks flush red. "I know you told me not to watch TV but I turned it on. I'm sorry. I'm sorry—I—" Lily bursts into tears and runs over to Otto and hugs his leg tightly. Sniffling and huffing Otto feels Lily grab his leg with every ounce of strength in her little body. "They said on the TV that they think that Sandy died. How could Sandy die? Why would someone hurt Sandy?"

Otto's heart drops as he puts his hand on Lily's little head as she hugs him tightly. First Lily's parents and now her best friend? How could so much tragedy happen to such a sweet young girl?

Otto looks up at his mother, unsure of what to do. Lily has only lived with Otto since she was three years old and he is still quite new to taking care of the child of his deceased best friend. It's not something you ask for. It's not something you will ever be prepared for. It's something you must do when you are called to help an innocent little girl who you know you can give an amazing life to after she suffered what no child should.

And losing her best friend is just another impossible blow.

"Well, sweetie, the police are still investigating," Bernice says as she rubs Lily's back. "All we can do is pray that it works out and that Sandy will get home safely. That's all we can do."

Otto bends down and picks up Lily, holding her up as she wraps her little legs around his torso.

"Look at me," Otto says softly as Lily covers her face. Lily peeks out slowly, just showing her little blue eyes in between her tiny fingers. "I am going to do everything in my power to bring Sandy back. Do you hear me? Even if I have to go find her myself. I promise you, Lily. I will do everything that I can."

· · · · · · · · ● · · · · · · · · · ·

Berlin's City Hall is not much of a city hall at all. It's more of a little brick building nestled up against the Androscoggin River. There are a few city offices, a rec department, and some other city services. Otto can't even imagine the last time city hall had a real media presence outside of it! Maybe never.

Nevertheless, he stands in front of a little wooden media podium outside of the little brick building as he stares into a sea of cameras staring back at him. He grips the podium as his hands shake. All eyes are on him.

Fox News, WMUR, *The Boston Globe, The Union Leader*— heck even CNN is here! Every media outlet wants to know why sweet little Sandy Sommers had gone missing.

In just the seventy-two hours since her disappearance on Easter Sunday, it has already become a national news story.

Podcasters were speculating that maybe it was her father who did it—he was divorced from her mother and had a history of drug use in his early twenties that at one point led him to a stint in the Coos County jail.

Others were speculating that it was Jeremy LeBlanc—a local sex offender who lived just up the street from the baseball park. When he was in his early twenties he went to prison for sexually assaulting a thirteen-year-old girl. Of course, he was in his late eighties now and under the care of an in-home nurse—but you just never knew.

Speculation was abundant.

When Otto became the mayor of Berlin, he always believed he was signing up for a relatively slow and calm time as the city's top executive. He wanted to build some new parks, bring more jobs to the community, and help the town find more purpose in their little mountain village. Now he was in the spotlight. Something he never wanted but something he would have to overcome to find Sandy Sommers.

Behind Otto stands the Berlin chief of police, Nolan Lavoie, who Otto suspects is woefully underprepared for this. Chief Lavoie is in his late fifties, waiting for retirement, and spends more time at the local Dunkin' Donuts than he does out in the field. His family has lived in Berlin since its founding in 1897 when the town was not much more than a few dirt roads in New Hampshire's north country. His family was the epitome of Coos County royalty. French Canadian, and so proud of their heritage that his parents still spoke Quebecois to this very day.

To the left of Chief Lavoie is a young Black woman named Clementine Miller. Otto doesn't really know much about her except that she's a special agent and had come up from Virginia for the press conference to assist with any questions from the media and to help solve the case.

Otto had never met an FBI agent before and he wasn't sure of the last time there was one in Berlin. While the town had its problems with drug abuse over the years like many other small cities in New Hampshire, Mayor Finch had implemented quite a few successful community-based programs that actually lowered the amount of illegal drug use in the county, helped more addicts find meaningful work, and reduced crime in the community.

Until Sandy disappeared, everything was going quite swimmingly in Berlin and for Mayor Finch's tenure. And poor Otto Finch is woefully unprepared for what is about to unravel in his little mountain town.

"Mr. Finch," says a young blond reporter from Fox News. "Our reporting shows that Mrs. Sommers was reportedly shopping when Sandy disappeared—is neglectful parenting being investigated as a factor in this case?"

Otto shakes his head and speaks into the microphone attached to the wooden podium in front of him. He's sweating through his suit as his voice shakes. "No, to my knowledge, Sandy was actually in the care of another parent at this time. It was an Easter egg hunt through the church and unfortunately, organizers lost track of Sandy at some point. We aren't sure when."

Another reporter interjects so quickly after the next question that Otto doesn't even have time to catch his breath.

"Mayor Finch, Catarina Love with WMUR, is it true that your daughter was at the Easter egg hunt with Sandy?"

Otto swallows hard as his stomach turns. "Yes. My daughter is best friends with Sandy. She didn't notice when Sandy slipped away from the crowd, but she was with her earlier in the day before it happened."

Another question comes like a firing squad as Otto grips the podium so tightly that his knuckles turn white.

"Hi, Mayor Finch, Ethel Flanagan with the *Conway Daily Sun*—what measures are you taking to ensure that your community is safe during this time?"

Otto clears his throat. "Well, starting today, Chief Lavoie and I have decided that there will be a sunset curfew for all unaccompanied children in Berlin. It's an easy step we can take until we bring Sandy home safely and ensure there is no more tragedy in our city."

CHAPTER 2

Otto can't sleep that night. He stares awake looking at the white ceiling in his bedroom, trying to rack his brain for anything he could do to help Sandy and in turn help Lily. The police had already done a full search of the fields, the woods, and the south side of Jericho Mountain. They turned up with nothing. Just a bit of evidence that Sandy had likely wandered off into the woods alone.

They were still searching. But according to the FBI and Chief Lavoie, it was becoming quite useless. They weren't making any progress and they would likely have to stop looking soon.

As Otto stared at the ceiling, he felt a familiar tug in his heart. A little voice in the back of his head. An unsettling feeling that something was wrong. *This doesn't happen in Berlin.*

Then again, in Otto's younger years, he had experienced terrifying things that you could never imagine were real! Years later, he wasn't sure if they were real but they certainly *felt real.*

Otto did his first year at university at Robin State College. He only spent his freshman year there for good reason. Something strange was happening in Robin at that time. Even now almost thirty years later, many people avoided Robin, with knowledge of what happened in the little community in 1998. Violence happened. Murder happened. What was once a small New Hampshire town erupted in a fit of seemingly unexplainable fury.

It was a full-blown riot.

And poor little Otto, who felt very alone and like a fish out of water just trying to survive—not only was he one of the only Black students on campus but he was queer to boot—and with black thick-rimmed glasses and a love for ornithology he felt more like the butt of a bad joke than a young man.

And then the violence started.

News outlets called it an instance of "mass hysteria." A strange "phenomenon." It began with the murder of one of the college's star baseball players and then it spiraled out of control from there. It got so evil and so violent that they no longer allow Halloween in Robin. You can't dress up. You can't go trick-or-treating. You can't even put a jack-o'-lantern on your front porch!

It was seemingly a small uneventful little New Hampshire town that turned into a nightmare. And Otto was there to see it all happen.

As he stares at the ceiling he wonders if it is happening again. Here, in Berlin. What if the evil followed him? What if Berlin is on the brink of violence?

Otto swallows hard and takes a deep breath.

He pushes the thought out of his brain and closes his eyes and counts backward from ten. It's a silly trick his therapist taught him. It's the only way he can stop his brain from spiraling this late at night.

Ten. Nine. Eight …

By six, the images start coming back. The ones his therapist said were just his mind's way of processing trauma. Distorted faces. People screaming. A creature's eyes turning yellow as it lunged at Otto with a broken bottle in its big, veiny hand. Five. Four …

The gaps in his memory that don't make sense. Whole days missing. Names he can't recall. His therapist called it dissociation—a normal response to trauma. But Otto always felt there was something more, something everyone was missing.

Three. Two …

The smell he couldn't forget. Like burnt matchsticks and rotten eggs. The way the air had felt heavy, like breathing through mud.

One.

Otto's eyes snap open. He reaches over to his bedside table, grabs the glass of water there and pauses when he sees the thin line of salt he'd sprinkled across the windowsill earlier that evening. His friends thought it was a bit strange. A superstition. But it was something he'd started doing after Robin that he couldn't explain even to himself. No matter the day, no matter the weather, no matter the moon, Otto always kept a thin line of salt at his bedroom windows. In Lily's too, though she often ruined it despite his warnings.

It was an important precaution.

Otto sits up in his bed, fully awake. His room looks the same as always—his work clothes laid out for tomorrow, the picture of his mother on the dresser, his books stacked nicely on his desk. But something feels off. The air is heavier. A chill runs through the room, making the hair on his arms stand on end.

He gets out of bed and walks to the window. Outside, the moonlight shines down on Jericho Mountain giving it a pale and unsettling glow. The forest where Sandy disappeared stretches dark and dense beyond the houses.

Otto touches the salt line, rubbing the crystals between his fingers. He should feel ridiculous—a grown man afraid of shadows. Yet the fear that clutches at his heart feels too real to dismiss. He can't remember it all, but the fragmented pieces of his memory are enough to leave him permanently disturbed.

"It's not happening again," he whispers to himself. "Sandy just wandered off. Kids get lost in these woods all the time."

But even as he says it, he knows it's not true. Kids don't just vanish into thin air. Not in Berlin.

Not unless something takes them.

Otto walks back to his bed and sits on the edge. He picks his phone up off of the nightstand and begins scrolling through his contacts until he finds a name he hasn't called in years. *Dr. Beatrix Brighton,* his old history professor from Robin. She was the only one who understood what he thought he'd seen during those terrible days.

His thumb hovers over her name. Would she even remember him? It's been decades, after all.

A cold gust of wind rattles his window, and Otto jumps, nearly dropping his phone. For just a moment, he thinks he sees something reflected in the glass. Something with bright amber eyes.

He blinks, and it's gone.

Otto presses call as his fingers shake.

He hopes she will answer. He prays she'll remember him. Most of all, he hopes she'll believe him when he tells her he's afraid it's all starting again. That whatever happened in Robin— whatever they never fully understood—has maybe found its way to Berlin.

That Sandy Sommers isn't just lost.

She's been taken.

Otto presses call and holds the phone to his ear. His heart pounds as it rings once, twice, three times.

Then, an automated voice. She sounds so old now. Her voice sounds sweet but cracked. "You've reached Dr. Beatrix

Brighton. I'm unavailable to take your call right now. Please leave a message after the tone."

The sound of her voice—even just a recording—sends a chill down Otto's spine. Memories flood back, fragmented and confusing. There's so much he wants to say. But he can't. His voice escapes him as silence fills his cold, dark bedroom.

What if she thinks he's crazy—she would never? But would she? He doesn't know her now. By his estimation—she's probably in her late sixties … maybe early seventies? What if she doesn't remember? What if someone else hears the message?

The beep sounds, and Otto freezes. He opens his mouth, but no words come out. After a few seconds of silence, he hangs up, his hand trembling.

He'll try again tomorrow. Maybe email her instead. Something less immediate, less desperate-sounding.

Otto lies back down and pulls the covers up to his chin as his hands begin to shake. He doesn't want to sleep. He doesn't want to close his eyes. But exhaustion pulls him under anyway.

When he sleeps, finally, in the small hours before dawn, his dreams are filled with pieces of dark memories. He's back at Robin State College. People are fighting in the quad. Someone is holding his hand, pulling him through the chaos, but when he turns to see who it is, the face blurs and fades.

"They're coming," this person says. "We have to stop them before they take anyone else."

And Otto wakes with a desperate gasp for air as he feels his cold T-shirt, drenched in sweat.

As he stares into the darkness of his bedroom, he knows one thing with absolute certainty: Sandy Sommers is in grave danger.

CHAPTER 3

The next morning, Otto wakes with ease. He didn't sleep that much anyway. In fact, he didn't really sleep at all. When he walks down the stairs from his bedroom and into the kitchen his mother is already standing over the stove, cooking her morning breakfast. It's early—just about six o'clock—and the sun has yet to rise, leaving the side of Jericho Mountain covered in darkness.

Lily sits at the kitchen table, already dressed in her school clothes, sipping on some orange juice. It is her first day back to school since her friend disappeared, and Otto can't imagine what is going through his daughter's head. She and Sandy did everything together. They sat next to each other in class, played together at recess. Thankfully Lily was starting to make other friends before Sandy's disappearance. She frequently mentioned a young girl named Gemma, though Otto had yet to meet her.

"What's for breakfast?" Otto asks as he walks over to Lily and kisses her on the forehead.

"Well, Grandma is making me some cereal and she's making you eggs. I don't like eggs," Lily says with a small frown.

"Well, that's a shame," Otto says. "Eggs will make you grow up big and strong!"

"I don't eat baby birds," Lily says with certainty.

"They're not baby birds!" Bernice says from the kitchen as she pushes the eggs around in the frying pan. "They are protein. Keep you full."

Lily crosses her arms across her chest. "Nope. Baby birds."

Otto smiles and rolls his eyes. On the kitchen table is a copy of the day's *Conway Daily Sun*. He picks it up with a careful eye and notices that he's on the front cover. It's a big picture of the press conference from yesterday with the headline: "Berlin Under Curfew as Authorities Search for Sandy Sommers." Otto's stomach turns. Another day of dealing with this nightmare. Maybe today he could pop across town to see Sandy's mom. He hadn't seen her since the day she went missing. She called him in a fit, begging him to start a search.

Something about the call made Otto feel uneasy. He couldn't put his finger on it. Maybe it's that Sandy's parents were known to have a lot of problems or maybe it was that Sandy's mom always had a new boyfriend in the house. Maybe Sandy's disappearance is *familial*.

"Dad," Lily says as she takes a big sip of her orange juice. "Can I ask you a question?"

Otto nods as he skims the paper. "Sure, sweetie."

26

"Would you come and wait for the bus with me today?" Lily asks as she looks down at her glass. "I don't want to wait there by myself."

Otto looks up from the paper and across the table at his daughter. "Of course, honey. With everything going on … I don't want you waiting anywhere by yourself. I will stand with you."

Usually in the morning, Otto would allow his daughter to take the short walk down the long dirt road to the end of the driveway by herself. He could see everything from the kitchen as clear as day through the long glass floor-to-ceiling windows that looked out over the property. But with everything going on, even that wasn't any assurance.

"Yeah, I think something is in the forest," Lily says, like it's no big deal. "I don't want to go near there anymore."

Otto's stomach turns.

Bernice stops cooking and walks toward the table, and Otto feels her leaning over him.

"What do you mean?" Otto asks.

Lily looks down and fidgets with her hands. "Well, when I was walking to the bus last week I think I saw something in the bushes."

"What did it look like?" Bernice asks.

Lily shrugs. "Well. At first I thought it was a dog. Until I realized it was too big to be a dog. It was white! Like a polar bear. But there're no polar bears in Berlin, are there?"

Otto shakes his head. "No, sweetie, not to my knowledge. The closest polar bears are very, very far north of us in Canada."

Lily nods and looks into her orange juice. "Yeah. I kind of figured it wasn't a polar bear because I heard it call my name."

Hearing Lily say that makes Otto feel sick. This can't be happening. Not here. Not to him. *Not to his family—or what little is left of it.*

"What did it say?" Otto asks with anger in his voice.

"Well. It said, '*Hi Lily*'—and it didn't come out from the bushes, but I could still see it had this big white face. And I told him that I was running late and I can't talk to strangers. So I ran to the bus as fast as I could."

"Was that last Tuesday? Is that why you were running up the road?" Bernice asks.

Lily nods.

"Sweetie, why didn't you say anything?" Bernice asked.

"Because I didn't think anyone would believe me."

CHAPTER 4

Otto is determined *not* to be like those other mayors in the horror movies who don't listen. The kind who ignore what their constituents are telling them. The kind who deny what they see with their own eyes. The kind of mayors that sweep everything under the rug and hope that everything turns out fine.

Instead, Otto is determined to take action without judgment. Sure, Lily is only six years old, and yes she has a very active imagination, but if she is right and something really is in the woods and if another child goes missing … he'll feel directly responsible.

When Otto walks into city hall that morning he quickly charges into his office, sits down at his desk, and picks up his phone.

A gruff voice picks up on the other line. "Chief Lavoie speaking. How can I help you?"

Otto grips the phone so tightly that he wonders if it's going to crack. "Chief Lavoie, I need you to send everyone back out in the field now. I need them to search the woods that run along the baseball field and up to where my house is at the base of Jericho Mountain."

Otto is met with silence on the other line.

"Hello? Chief? Are you there?"

"Yes, Mayor Finch, I'm here." Apathy seeps through the microphone.

"I need you to send out as many officers as you can, ASAP. A full search and rescue."

"Mayor—the guys just got back after being out for seventy-two hours and found nothing. I can't send them back out there. They're absolutely exhausted."

Otto's voice shakes with anger. "I need you to send them back out."

"Why?"

His forehead is sweating now. He can't tell the chief that his daughter saw something in the woods. No one will listen to a six-year-old. So Otto swallows hard and he does what he absolutely hates for any politician to do—he lies.

"I saw something, in the woods by the house," Otto says as his voice shakes.

Chief Lavoie's tone evolves from apathetic to interested. "What did you see?"

Otto racks his brain quickly trying to think of something that's not too strange. "I um—I saw a man. Walking through the woods. And he looked deranged."

"How so?"

"Like he was angry. His hair was all scruffed up and there was blood on his shirt."

"Blood on his shirt?"

Otto felt a pang in his stomach when he realized that he was *technically* committing a felony by lying to a police officer. But if it brought back Sandy … it would all be worth it.

"Yes! Blood on his shirt. And he had a knife!"

"A knife? Did he look like a vagrant? Did he look like he was living in the woods? What else did he look like?"

"I'm not sure. I couldn't get a good enough look."

"You think he's violent?"

Otto shrugs his shoulders and swallows hard. "Um … maybe?"

"And when did you see him?"

"This morning. On my way to the office."

Chief Lavoie takes a deep breath and sighs. "Alright. We'll send some of the team back out."

• • • • • • • • • ● • • • • • • • • • •

Otto knows that it is a bit irresponsible—forcing the chief of police to send everyone back out into the field chasing a person who doesn't exist—but if it helps find Sandy, it was all worth it.

31

After getting off the phone with Chief Lavoie, Otto makes his way to the other side of Berlin to a little apartment complex on the border of West Milan. It's a three-story building with white siding that is slowly falling apart. Pieces of the siding are strewn on the ground and one of the windows is broken on the lower level. Outside a few beat-up cars sit parked in the muddy lot. There are a lot of buildings like this in Berlin, and since becoming mayor, Otto has made it his mission to reinvest back in the community so Berlin can be a place of community pride. A shining little city nestled in the White Mountains.

But it's not easy.

With very few jobs and little to look forward to … most of Berlin was quite sad. And with a little girl gone missing, things were about to get even more grim.

He knocks on the door of the apartment on the third floor, while standing on a wooden porch that serves as a connector to the different floors of the apartment. He hears a bit of rustling inside and then steps toward the door.

When it opens, Sandy's mom, Sarah Sommers, stands in front of him with big bloodshot eyes. With dark circles hanging under them, she looks like she hasn't slept in days. She wears an oversized shirt that falls below her knees and no pants.

"Otto," Sarah says as her voice shakes. She's a young mom who had Sandy when she was in high school and Otto is in his forties, so even though their children were friends, they didn't have much in common. Most of their communication is reduced to scheduling time for the girls to spend together. But at this moment, Otto feels deeply connected to Sarah for the first time. They both understand loss.

Otto pulls Sarah in for a hug and holds her tightly as she begins to sob.

"I'm so sorry, Sarah," Otto says as he rubs her back. "I promise I will do everything in my power to bring Sandy home to you. I promise."

Otto sits at the kitchen table inside Sarah's little apartment. He wraps his hands around the big warm mug of coffee that Sarah made him. It's probably Folgers or something similar. It's acidic and grainy when it hits Otto's tongue and he instantly assumes that either Sarah's taste buds are nonexistent or she is not much of a coffee person.

But at least it's warming his hands.

The little apartment is freezing on the inside. The oven is cracked open leaving a little draft of heat to spill into the kitchen. Otto remembers those days. Growing up, his family didn't have much and his mother always kept the oven door open on the cold winter nights in Berlin. And it got cold. Below freezing in the depths of winter with just a glimmer of sunlight to make the long days somewhat bearable.

Sarah sits across from Otto with her head in her hands. "I just keep telling myself that it can't be real. That this can't be happening. That I am just going to wake up one morning and

Sandy is going to run into my room and jump on my bed like any other day. I just can't believe this."

Otto nods and reaches for her hand across the table. He squeezes it lightly. "I am going to do everything that I can to help you. I promise, Sarah."

Sarah nods as a tear rolls down her cheek.

"You know, I came by to check on you but I also came by to ask you a few questions if you don't mind."

Sarah nods slowly.

"Can we just keep this conversation between us?" Otto asks. "I kind of … don't really know what to make of it."

"Is everything OK?"

"I don't know," Otto says. He pulls his hand away and puts it back on the mug, fiddling with the handle. "I don't want to alarm you but I think something strange is going on in Berlin right now. With Sandy's disappearance—it's just not normal."

Sarah nods and narrows her eyes. "What are you trying to say?"

"What I am trying to say is—maybe something is going on here. Lily told me that she saw something in the woods by our house. And that it spoke to her."

Sarah leans in and shifts in her seat.

"She said that she was walking to the bus stop one morning and that there was something in the bushes that talked to her. And knew her name. I don't know if it was a man or a woman or anything like that. But that's what she told me this morning. Has Sandy mentioned anything similar to you?"

Sarah shakes her head. "No. Not to my knowledge. But I can ask her father. She has a bit of a different relationship with him if that makes sense."

Otto nods. "That would be great."

"Actually on second thought," Sarah says as she cocks her head to the side, "one of the girls I work with mentioned something last week."

"At the hospital?"

"Yeah, there's this nurse I work with, Clara. She told me a story that I thought was a bit strange."

Sarah pauses, rubbing at her temples like she's trying to shake loose the memory. "She told me that her son—he's around fifteen—he said something weird to her the other night. He told her that he met someone in the woods."

Otto's stomach clenches. "Met someone?"

Sarah nods slowly. "Yeah. Out by the mountain."

The kitchen suddenly feels smaller, the air thick. Otto grips the coffee mug tighter, but it's gone cold in his hands.

"Did he say what he looked like?" Otto asks, his voice barely above a whisper.

Sarah looks up at him, her expression unreadable. "He said the man was hiding in the bushes and knew his name. Talked to him like a friend."

CHAPTER 5

Otto's phone ring breaks the silence of Sarah's small apartment. It's so loud that it makes his heart race. He looks down at his iPhone that sits on Sarah's kitchen table and it glows with a familiar name—Chief Lavoie.

Sarah sees the name light up from across the table and her eyes shine with a glimmer of hope.

Otto picks up the phone quickly. "Hey, Chief, what's going on?"

"I have some good news for you," says Chief Lavoie in his gruff and grainy voice. "I don't think we're going to have to send another group out into the woods after all."

Otto frowns. "And why is that?"

"Well, a hunter was out behind your house this morning and he found two kids—teenagers—who matched the exact description you gave us this morning. They were at the base of the mountain. Both of them were carrying hunting knives. Their sweatshirts were drenched in blood. When the hunter approached them, he said that they were too stunned to speak. Two of 'em were just sitting on a tree stump staring into the distance. Must have been on some hard shit."

Otto's stomach turns. Behind his house?

How could they find people who matched Otto's description when he had made the details up?

"We are bringing them in for questioning now. Do you want to meet us at the station? I have a feeling that they know something about what happened to Sandy."

· · · · · · ●●● ● ●●●●● · · · ·

When Otto arrives at the police station it's buzzing with activity. What has typically been a sleepy quiet outpost for the city's law enforcement has turned into a bustling headquarters for Sandy's rescue. The little brick building off Main Street is swarming with law enforcement from other cities, the state, and even the federal government.

As Otto walks into the station and toward the back of the building where Chief Lavoie's office is, police officers giving Otto a nod of acknowledgment as he walks by.

"Thank you for all your hard work," Otto says as he weaves through the crowd of bodies that have clogged the open part of the office. "I know we are going to find her. I feel it in my bones."

When he finally reaches the back of the room, Chief Lavoie is coming out of his office. The man's big belly exits the office first as he walks up to Otto carrying a glazed chocolate donut in one hand and an extra-large Dunkin' Donuts cup in the other hand.

"You ready for this, Boston?" Chief Lavoie says as a smile erupts across his face.

Otto rolls his eyes. He can't stand Lavoie's patronizing nickname. It's one of the few things he can't stand about Berlin. When Otto was a young man, he left his home to make something of himself. To learn. To expand his knowledge and skill set. His goal was always to bring that experience back to Berlin, but every now and then someone would make an offhanded comment— "Boston," "Mayor Fancy Pants," "Harvard"—it would make his stomach turn. Maybe they were jealous. Maybe they harbored some sort of resentment against him. But Otto only had the best and purest interests at heart—making Berlin the best that it could be for everyone who lives there.

"I'm sure I can handle it," Otto says as he follows Chief Lavoie down a long hallway filled with offices. Toward the end are the interrogation rooms. Otto has never been in an interrogation room before. He's only seen them on television— never in real life. Of course, he wasn't being interrogated, but a small part of him still felt nervous.

What if these two teenage boys hurt Sandy? What if they killed her? Otto can't bear the thought. It's been days though. If Sandy *is* alive wandering in the woods by herself—she probably won't survive that much longer on her own.

Chief Lavoie leads Otto to a room at the end of the hall. "You go in here," Lavoie says as he opens the door showing Otto into a small room with one-way glass. Clementine, the FBI agent from the press conference is sitting in the room on the other side of the glass, scrolling through her phone.

"Special Agent Miller and I will be conducting the interrogation; you just sit here and look pretty. And do not interfere. Do you understand me?" Chief Lavoie says as his brow furrows. He points to a small chair in the corner of the observation room. "This could take a few hours. You're welcome to stay as little or as long as you'd like. And whatever you hear, don't say a word to anyone outside of these four walls. Do you understand?"

"Yes I understand, I'm not a child—I—"

"Good," Chief Lavoie says. He slams the door behind him leaving Otto alone in the dark observation room that is lit up only by the fluorescent lights of the interrogation room.

Otto takes a seat in the wooden chair in the corner and watches through the one-way glass as Clementine scrolls through her phone, waiting for the interrogation to start.

Otto wonders what she thinks of Berlin. If she feels comfortable here. Otto joined the Black Student Union when he got to Northeastern; after growing up in Berlin and struggling through Robin State, where he counted the other Black students on one hand. Having a real community felt like exhaling a breath he'd held his whole life.

He met Ty at one of their Friday mixers—tall, track-built, with a Georgia drawl that melted every word. The track star from Georgia Tech lingered by the drinks table, looking both in and out of place, like Otto always felt.

"You dodging the crowd too?" Ty had asked, passing him a red cup. "I hate this kind of networking! Shit … But I guess it's all part of the college experience. Are you new to BSU too?"

Three hours later, they were still talking. Two weeks later, they were inseparable.

On Christmas of their second year, Otto made the mistake of bringing Ty home. He wanted to show off Berlin—his Berlin—the snow-hushed mountains and twilight that lasted all afternoon.

The Dunkin' Donuts on Main Street told them everything they needed to know. Otto pushed open the door, bell jingling, and the place didn't exactly go silent—it was worse than that. Conversations lowered, necks craned, spoons stirred coffee with sudden concentration.

"Good morning, Mrs. Lapierre." Otto nodded to his third-grade teacher, whose smile tightened as her eyes darted between him and Ty.

Later, trudging back through the snow, Ty laughed hoarsely. "Your coffee really is different up here."

But Otto saw how Ty's shoulders hunched inside his coat, how his eyes swept each room they entered, calculating exits, threats, judgments.

The Hannaford cashier who suddenly needed to "check inventory" when they approached her line. The gas station attendant who looked past Ty to ask Otto if he was "showing your friend around our little town?" with a smile that didn't reach his eyes.

Their third night, they lay in Otto's childhood bed, staring at the glow-in-the-dark stars he'd stuck on the ceiling in fifth grade.

"Everyone knows you," Ty said, his voice quiet in the dark.

Otto turned on his side. "But?"

Ty smiled, but his eyes stayed fixed on the plastic stars. "But they look at me like I'm from fucking Mars, man." He finally turned to face Otto. "Like they've never seen Black people before."

They lasted four more months after that trip. The breakup had other reasons—Ty's residency in Atlanta, Otto's commitment to Berlin—but Otto never forgot the look in Ty's eyes, that slow realization that the town Otto loved had no space carved out for someone like him.

The interrogation room door swung open, breaking Otto's thoughts. Chief Lavoie lumbered in, and Clementine straightened, tucking her phone away. They spoke briefly before Lavoie checked his watch with a frown.

"Twenty-minute delay," he announced, sticking his head into the observation room. "Some paperwork mess with the juveniles."

Before he could think better of it, Otto was out the door, catching Clementine in the hallway.

"Special Agent Miller?"

She turned, one eyebrow raised. "Mayor Finch."

"This might seem forward, but would you like to join us for dinner tonight? My mother makes a pot roast that'll make you forget every bad diner meal you've had since you got here." Otto felt heat creep up his neck. "Lily would love the company. And I thought you might appreciate something that isn't takeout."

Clementine studied him, her face professional, unreadable. Then, a slow smile broke through.

"That's actually really kind," she said. "I've been living on gas station coffee and vending machines."

"Eight too late?"

"Eight's perfect." She nodded once. "And it's Clementine."

"Otto," he replied.

As she walked away, Otto turned to find Chief Lavoie watching from the doorway, eyebrows nearly at his hairline.

"What?" Otto challenged.

Lavoie's mouth twitched into that smirk Otto had wanted to wipe off his face since high school. "Ah, ben," he drawled with that Quebecois lilt that always crept in when he was amused. "C'est tout, là? That's all, Boston? Just dinner?"

CHAPTER 6

Kyle Gauthier had never been inside a police station, never mind inside of an interrogation room. In fact, Kyle had never gotten himself into any kind of trouble whatsoever. He was a straight-A student, soccer team varsity captain at Berlin High School, and the president of the FBLA (Future Business Leaders of America) chapter.

Now he's sitting in handcuffs in a small interrogation room in the back of the Berlin Police Department. He's across from a young Black woman in her mid-thirties with a stern but kind expression, and a fat, old, white cop whose stomach looks like it's about to bust out of his shirt, sending his buttons rocketing across the room.

"Hi, Mr. Gauthier. I am Special Agent Clementine Miller with the FBI, and this is Chief Lavoie; he is the head of the Berlin Police Department," she says as she sticks out her hand.

Kyle stares at her delicate hand in the middle of the table. His stomach twists and turns as he tries to rack his brain for how he got here. He doesn't remember much, but when he looks down at his bloodstained shirt he remembers something. Pain. Anxiety. He remembers being terrified.

He looks down at his hands that are covered in mud and dirt. If only Kyle could remember the past twenty-four hours, he'd feel a whole lot better.

"Sorry, my hands are super dirty," Kyle says as he shows Agent Miller.

"No worries," she says, letting out a small smile. "Were you able to get ahold of your parents? Are they coming?"

Kyle shakes his head and before he can open his mouth Chief Lavoie lays his fat meaty hands on the table with a loud *thud*.

"That's OK!" Chief Lavoie says. "Don't need them anyway. Just need to ask you a quick few questions and then we can send you on your way. The more you hem and haw, the more you dilly-dally, the longer we will be here and the harder this will be for you."

"You don't need to scare him," Agent Miller says as her face turns into a frown. "He's most likely completely innocent, right, Kyle?"

Kyle's eyes widen. He shouldn't be here. He should be home with his dog and his mom watching television. It's right around the time that he usually comes home from school and his mom is waiting with an afternoon snack. Where is she? Why isn't she picking up the phone? Kyle can't remember anything at this point.

"Why were you in the woods at the edge of Jericho Mountain?" Chief Lavoie growls.

"I don't remember," Kyle says. "Am I being investigated for some sort of crime? I don't understand."

"Have you seen this girl?" Chief Lavoie asks as he picks up a paper from the table and holds up a sweet little picture of a young girl just about six years old.

Kyle shakes his head. "No, I mean—I don't think so."

His eyes dart between the FBI agent and the police chief, his confusion probably evident. "I really don't know why I was out there. The last thing I remember clearly was being at home, doing homework … then everything gets fuzzy."

Chief Lavoie leans forward, his chair creaking under his weight. "Fuzzy how? You just happened to wander into the woods with blood all over your clothes? That's quite a sleepwalking episode."

"I don't know," Kyle says, his voice cracking. He looks down at his dirty hands again. "I remember the pain. Like my head was splitting open. I've never felt anything like it before. That's all I really remember."

"Well, we checked you out. No bumps and bruises on you. You're fine," Lavoie says. "Someone else can't say the same."

Agent Miller's tone softens. "Take your time, Kyle. Anything you can remember might help us."

Kyle closes his eyes, concentration etched on his face. "I mean ... I guess I remember that there was this ... tunnel? I think? It was dark, but not completely. Like there was a little light way off in the distance."

"A tunnel?" Chief Lavoie scoffs. "There aren't any tunnels in those woods."

"I'm trying my best. I'm trying to remember. I want to help, I—"

"It's OK," Agent Miller says. "Just keep going. Try your best."

Kyle nods and closes his eyes again. "I remember walking down it. Johnny and I thought it was cool—we wanted to see what was at the end. But I was ... I was scared. Really scared. Johnny wanted to keep going but I didn't. I wanted to turn around and go home. And then we began to hear things."

"What kind of things?" Agent Miller asks.

"Like something else was down there," Kyle says. "We thought maybe it was like a mountain lion or something so we pulled out our knives."

"Ain't no mountain lions on Jericho," Chief Lavoie grumbles.

Agent Miller shoots a cautionary glance at Lavoie before continuing. "What happened next, Kyle?"

"That's just it—I don't know. The next thing I remember is waking up in the woods. Johnny was there too, looking just as confused as me. We were both covered in dirt and"—he looks down at his stained clothes—"this. Then this hunter found us, started yelling. Screaming, even, and now I'm here."

"You expect us to believe you have no idea how you got blood all over yourself?" Chief Lavoie demands, his face reddening.

"I swear I don't!" Kyle's eyes fill with tears. "I've never even been hunting. I've never hurt anything in my life! You can ask my teachers, my coaches … ask anyone!"

"What about Johnny?" Agent Miller interjects. "Did he say anything about how you both ended up there?"

Kyle shakes his head. "He's just as freaked out as me—we were just sitting on the stump trying to remember until that hunter came. He kept asking me what happened, but I didn't know either."

"Convenient," Chief Lavoie mutters.

"Please," Kyle says, looking directly at Agent Miller, his handcuffs rattling as he shifts in his seat. "I'm scared. I don't understand what's happening. I want my mom. I want to go home."

Agent Miller exchanges a glance with Chief Lavoie. "Kyle, we're going to need to run some tests on your clothes. We'll also need to speak with Johnny and compare your stories."

"Tests?" Kyle's eyes widen. "You think that's … you think that's someone's blood? Oh God." His face turns pale as his stomach turns. Sweat runs down his forehead in pools. "Is this about that missing little girl? I would never hurt a kid! Never!"

Chief Lavoie stands up abruptly. "We'll be back in a few minutes. Don't go anywhere." He chuckles darkly at his own joke, gesturing to the handcuffs.

As they exit, Kyle calls out, his voice breaking, "Please call my mom again! Please!"

The door closes with a heavy thud, leaving Kyle alone in the observation room staring down at his bloodstained shirt.

CHAPTER 7

Otto doesn't leave the police station until early evening. Watching every minute of Kyle and Johnny's interrogation was his top priority. And once the questioning was concluded and it was time to call it for today, Otto quickly left the station and hopped into his black Jeep Wrangler and rocketed off toward the house.

The interrogation rattled Otto to his core. He grips the wheel of his Jeep so tight that his knuckles turn white as he weaves through downtown Berlin. There's something about their stories that Otto can't shake. He resonates with them. He feels them. He knows what it is like for no one to believe you. For people to think that you're crazy. For the police, the "grown-ups" and everyone around you to question your sanity.

When Johnny was interrogated, his answers were almost identical to Kyle's.

Johnny didn't know what happened.

He didn't remember much.

He remembered being in pain. Deep pain.

And the tunnel … Johnny remembered the tunnel in even greater detail than Kyle. He described how the tunnel was humid and muddy and made sharp turns—seeming to go on forever.

Chief Lavoie quickly wrote off the tunnel.

He asked the boys if they were doing hard drugs. LSD. Meth. Heroin.

As Otto watched through the one-way glass, taking notes on his iPhone, he studied every word that the boys said. They couldn't remember where the tunnel was, but they described the entrance as a big gaping hole. A mouth, etched into a small hill, descending into the cool darkness. They said it was behind a thick layer of brush and that the tunnel went on for miles.

While Chief Lavoie berated the boys, Otto watched with intent, knowing one thing for certain: He had to find the tunnel. No matter what.

· · · · · · · · ● · · · · · · · · ·

When Otto opens the door to his house he is greeted by a creature. A large, gray and lanky beast almost bigger than Otto. His name is Tiny and he's one of Bernice's Irish wolfhounds. She just so happens to have four of them. If you've never seen an Irish wolfhound before, they look like a real-life werewolf. A lanky, athletic beast that is often used and bred for hunting— and that's exactly what Bernice did. In fact, Bernice was one of the premiere Irish wolfhound breeders on the Eastern Seaboard.

It wasn't something she did when Otto was a child, but once he was off at college, her husband came home one day with a bundle of fur that could barely fit in his arms. Herb Finch had found the sickly wolfhound pup abandoned by the side of the road near the paper mill. Despite the pup's mangy appearance, Bernice nursed the dog back to health, feeding him every two hours through the night, mixing special formulas, and even sleeping on the floor next to his makeshift bed.

They named him Kobe, after the Lakers rookie who Harold had taken a liking to while watching games that winter. "That boy's going to be a star," he'd predicted, "and so is this dog." Harold's basketball predictions usually came true, and this one was no exception—both for the player and the pup. As Kobe grew—seemingly by inches every day—so did Bernice's fascination with the breed.

Bernice had always been a practical woman with practical interests, but something about these gentle giants captured her imagination. She began subscribing to wolfhound magazines, joining online forums, and traveling to shows across New England to learn everything she could.

Herb would tell anyone who would listen that he'd never seen his wife so passionate about anything outside of raising Otto. When Bernice started talking about breeding, their small ranch house on Pine Street became suddenly, impossibly cramped.

That's when Otto, freshly graduated and working at his first real estate development job in Boston, decided to put his skills to use for his family. He found the perfect property at the foot of Mount Cabot—three acres with enough room for the dogs to run, a modest but solid house that he could renovate, and most importantly, enough space to build proper kennels.

Otto still remembered the look on his mother's face when he showed her the property. The way her eyes had lit up as she walked the land, already planning where the whelping room would go, where the exercise yard would be, how she'd arrange the kennels to catch the morning sun.

"You sure about this, son?" Herb had asked, knowing what a financial stretch it would be for Otto.

"More sure than I've been about anything," Otto had replied.

Within five years, Finch wolfhounds had produced two national champions. Bernice had found her calling late in life, but she'd found it with a vengeance. After Herb passed away from a sudden heart attack, the dogs became more than a passion—they were her salvation, her purpose, her community.

And now, as Tiny's massive paws landed on Otto's shoulders in greeting, three more wolfhounds appeared in the hallway, their tails creating a tornado of wagging excitement.

Otto stumbles into the kitchen, dog hair coating his suit pants. The dogs didn't bother Bernice—she just hollers "Get down, ya beasts!" without turning from her cutting board.

"You look like shit," she tells him, knife thwacking through roast beef.

"Thanks, Ma."

"Not a compliment." Her wrist never stops its rhythm. Chop-slide-chop. She'd been cutting meat that way since Otto was a boy, her bun tight at the nape of her neck, now more gray than black but still no-nonsense. Seventy years hasn't slowed her hands.

"Lily's upstairs. She's resting. Today has been really hard for her. I think she was finally able to take a nap."

Otto drops onto a chair that had survived three decades of Finch family dinners. The table has cigarette burns from when his father still smoked, water rings from forgotten drinks, scratches from homework and tax returns and arguments.

Bernice looks up, knife mid-slice. Her eyes narrow.

"Mom, you have no idea how horrible today has been."

"I can imagine," she mutters. The knife clatters against the cutting board. She wipes her fingers on a dish towel hanging from her apron string, moves to the cabinet, and pulls down Otto's whiskey. The good stuff, hidden behind cereal boxes where Lily won't reach it.

She never measures, just pours till it feels right, then puts the glass on the table in front of Otto.

"Drink," she orders, pulling out a chair. The legs scrape against linoleum. "Then talk."

•••••••••●•••••••••

Bernice's eyes widen when Otto tells her about the tunnel. It's one of his favorite things about his mother—she's not judgmental. She's not critical. She just listens.

"So, what are you saying?" Bernice asks as she listens to Otto hanging on every single word even though she's chopping up vegetables to prepare for dinner.

"I'm saying," Otto says as he takes a long sip of his whiskey. "I'm saying that I think there's a tunnel in Jericho Mountain." Otto lowers his voice into a whisper. "And I think that's where Sandy is."

Bernice nods but before she can utter a word, the doorbell rings. Her eyes widen. "Are you expecting anyone?"

Otto frowns and then he remembers. "Shit. Yes! Oh my Gosh. I am so sorry."

"Sorry?"

Otto springs up from his seat. "I invited this woman over for dinner."

Bernice let's out a small smile. "Woman?"

Otto shakes his head. "No, Ma, it's not like that. You know it's not like that."

Bernice shrugs her shoulders. "I don't judge. But you did hop up awfully quick like she matters quite a lot to you."

"One minute!" Otto yells into the large echoing house. He turns to Bernice. "She is a special agent with the FBI and she's up here all alone from Virginia. I figured she could use some community. Berlin is not an easy place to be."

CHAPTER 8

Otto watches as Tiny sprawls out beneath the dining room table, his massive head resting directly at Agent Miller's feet. The dog's big brown eyes are locked on her plate with an intensity that makes Otto smile despite everything weighing on his mind.

"Your dogs are beautiful—I've never seen anything like them!" Agent Miller says, clearly impressed by the gentle giants.

Otto notices how comfortable she looks at their dining room table, more relaxed than he's seen her since she arrived in Berlin. The formal FBI agent from the interrogation room has softened here in his home, among his family and his mother's cooking.

"Tiny is my favorite," Lily pipes up, her voice small but clear.

Otto turns to look at his daughter, relief washing through him at the sound of her voice. She's been pushing food around her plate all evening, barely engaging, barely present. This is the first time she's looked up during dinner, the first spark of the vibrant little girl he knows. The disappearance of her friend has dimmed her light, and Otto has been desperate to see even a flicker of it return.

His mother catches his eye from across the table, a silent communication passing between them. She sees it too—this tiny moment of connection, of normalcy. They are both clinging to it.

"This food is delicious," Agent Miller says as she takes another bite of her roast beef. "I have been exclusively eating horrible takeout for the past three days so I really appreciate it. And I have to ask—is there any good food around here? I mean—*really good food.*"

Otto lets out a small smile. There's not much variety up here in the mountains. "I mean, what do you like?"

"Literally anything besides a burger and french fries."

Otto looks at his mother across the table who lets out a small smile.

Agent Miller laughs. "I'm shit out of luck aren't I?"

"I mean, there are a few little pubs downtown that are pretty solid. O'Malley's has good nachos," Bernice says.

"Yeah, it's kind of slim pickings. But if you drive down a bit west toward Lancaster you'll have a few more options," Otto says. "But I am sure you're a bit busy."

Agent Miller nods and takes a sip of her wine.

While Otto is enjoying her company, he feels such restraint at the same time. He wants to talk to her so badly. Open and freely. He wants to ask her about the tunnel. What their plan is—are they even going to go look?

Of course, he can't say any of this in front of little Lily whose expression looks like a deflated balloon.

"How was school today?" Otto asks his daughter, trying his best to engage her in the conversation.

She shrugs her shoulders and pushes her food around her plate with her fork. "It stunk."

"I'm sorry, sweetie, and why is that?" asks Bernice.

"They won't let us go outside for recess because of what happened to Sandy. So we just sat inside all day. I love recess," Lily says as a long sigh escapes her.

"I'm sorry, that must be really hard," Otto says.

Silence fills the room as Lily returns to pushing her peas around her plate. "May I be excused?"

"Are you sure, sweetie? You've barely eaten."

Lily nods.

"Alright," Otto says softly. "Just make sure to put your plate in the sink."

Lily slides off her chair, and her little feet land softly on the hardwood floor. As she walks past Agent Miller, she pauses.

"Are you going to find Sandy?" The question comes out barely above a whisper.

Agent Miller sets down her fork. The warmth and relaxation that had softened her features moments before harden into something more professional.

"We're doing everything we possibly can," she says, the careful words of someone who knows better than to make promises.

Lily's small shoulders slump almost imperceptibly. "That's what everyone says."

She carries her plate to the sink, the scrape of utensils against ceramic the only sound in the suddenly still room. Tiny follows her, his massive form shadowing her tiny one, as if understanding she needs protection.

When she reaches the doorway, Lily turns back. "I'm going to draw a picture of Sandy. For when she comes home. So she knows I didn't forget her."

Otto feels his throat tighten. "That's a wonderful idea, sweetie."

After Lily disappears upstairs, Bernice clears her throat and reaches for the wine bottle. "More for anyone?"

Otto watches the doorway where his daughter had stood, wondering how to help her carry a grief too heavy for her small shoulders. From upstairs comes the sound of a drawer opening and closing, followed by the soft crinkle of paper.

"She draws a new picture every night," Bernice says quietly to Agent Miller. "Puts them in a folder under her bed. Says she's going to give them all to Sandy when she comes back."

CHAPTER 9

Lily is irritated. But she doesn't want any of the grown-ups in the dining room to know it. For the past three days, they've been telling her that they're doing "everything in their power to find Sandy." If that's true, why are they sitting around a table laughing and drinking like nothing ever happened?

Like Lily's best friend hasn't disappeared forever?

If they won't find Sandy, Lily will have to take matters into her own hands.

Little did the grown-ups know, Lily had been eavesdropping on every word of their conversation before the FBI agent came for dinner. While Otto and Bernice talked about Sandy's disappearance, Lily was hiding right around the corner, watching them drink whiskey and talk about the boys who had been arrested earlier that day.

Lily listened to every single word.

And she came to a similar conclusion as her father. *There must be tunnels in the woods and Sandy has to be in there. If* these "adults" want to sit around and gossip all night instead of working to find her friend, then Lily must take matters into her own hands! That's what a best friend should do.

After dinner, Lily quickly runs up to her room to prepare. She puts on her bright yellow galoshes, her long winter coat, and grabs the flashlight that she keeps beside her bed to walk to the bathroom at night. She empties out her yellow Bluey backpack and grabs some water from the upstairs pantry and some snacks. Who knows how long she will be gone?

But Lily knows one thing for certain—*Sandy is alive.* She can't explain why or how she knows this but she can feel it in her bones. Her best friend in the world is sitting out there in those tunnels all by herself. She's probably scared, frightened, and hungry! Lily throws an extra sweater in her backpack—when she finds Sandy, she will probably be very cold. The forest is freezing at night and she's been out there for days.

Once Lily gathers all her things, she opens the window to her bedroom and lets the cold winter air breeze through the house. This isn't the first time that she's escaped in the middle of the night without her father or grandmother knowing. In fact, Lily loves to wander off in the middle of the night when they're asleep. There's something so relaxing about the woods at night.

But tonight is different.

Tonight, Lily is on a clear mission—to find Sandy. At all costs.

When Lily's little feet hit the ground, the green spring grass catches her shoes like a pillow. The hardest part about leaving at night isn't climbing down from her window—it's doing her best to get as far away from the house without tipping off one of the dogs. Tiny, Simba, Cleo, and Rufus often sit in the dining room at this time, looking out at the big glass window in the dining room that shows a view of the forest.

One time, when Lily was wandering out at night, the dogs saw her walking on the edge of the forest and they barked so much they almost had a fit! Little Lily ran back toward the house, climbed up to her window and quickly snuck into her bed before anyone could notice. It scared her, and ever since, Lily was extra cautious to sneak right around the house, outside of the sight of the dogs, and as far out of view as she could be from anyone watching in the windows.

The dark edge of the forest looms over her as she walks quietly closer to it. Lily isn't afraid of the forest. Even though it is dark and scary and home to terrifying creatures, Lily always feels oddly safe.

She feels safe because she had a friend there.

Lily doesn't know his name or anything about him really—just that sometimes he will sit on the edge of the forest and talk to her. Lily's friend has a few rules to their friendship though that she was mostly OK with: she isn't allowed to see him, she isn't allowed to tell her father, and she isn't allowed to ask him any personal questions.

Other than that, they have a great friendship.

His voice is soothing to her in a strange way. Like a big brother or a father. They first met about a year ago when Lily was out playing in the backyard by herself.

Lily was hunting four-leaf clovers when she first heard it. A voice, soft as wind chimes, drifting from the shadows where her yard melted into forest.

"Pretty dress, Lily."

She froze. Her dad's warnings about strangers flashed through her mind, but this voice … it didn't scare her. It felt like when Mrs. Pelletier at kindergarten read stories during circle time—warm and safe.

"Thank you," she called back, squinting at the trees. "Who's there?"

"Just a friend. I live here. I've been watching you hunt for clovers. You're going to need more than luck to find a four-leafer."

Lily took three careful steps toward the woods. "Come out of the woods. Can I see you?"

"No, Lily. Can't do that." Something rustled in the underbrush. "I'm shy. And I've got … well … I've got a bit of a condition. Let's say I look a little different. Scares folks. But I'd sure like to be friends, if that's OK?"

Lily scrunched her face, thinking. Dad always said trust your gut. Her gut said this was OK.

"What do I call you?"

Silence stretched so long she thought maybe he'd gone away. Then: "Call me BFF."

Lily burst into giggles. "That's silly! Sandy's my BFF. I can't have two."

The voice laughed—a sound like hot cocoa tastes. "Of course you can. I've had lots in my time."

After that, Lily started sneaking to the edge of the yard. BFF taught her which berries were poisonous, which trees were oldest, which animal made which tracks. He listened to her problems—real problems—not like grown-ups who just pretended.

"Tell me about Sandy," he'd asked once. "What makes her so special?"

"She gives me her cookies at lunch," Lily had said, picking at grass stems. "And when I said *pacific* instead of *specific* in class, she didn't laugh like Ally did. That's why she's my BFF."

"Best friend forever," BFF had whispered, like he was tasting the words. "That's what it means, right? Your BFF?"

Lily cocked her head. "Well, yeah. What's it mean to you?"

The woods had gone quiet—that special quiet that feels loud somehow.

"Best forest friend," he'd finally said, voice dropping deeper. "'Cause I'll be watching you from these trees. Always."

Something in those words sent cold spiders crawling up her back, but Lily pushed the feeling down. Two BFFs are twice as good as one, even if one was just a voice.

For months, they'd talked this way. Never seeing, never telling, never asking personal stuff. Those were the rules. Lily mostly didn't mind, though sometimes she'd lie awake wondering what he really looked like.

Soon after, he disappeared.

Twice she'd gone to their spot, called his name. Nothing. Just wind and leaves. The first time, she figured he was busy. The second time, she waited forever, calling till her throat hurt.

That was right before Sandy vanished.

Now, stepping into the midnight forest, Lily hugged herself against the cold. Her flashlight made monsters out of tree shadows. She needed to find Sandy. And maybe BFF could help—nobody knew these woods better.

"BFF?" she whispered. "Please? I need you. Sandy's gone." Her voice echoes through the woods, bouncing back to her.

Nothing answers but an owl, somewhere far away.

Something sick and heavy settles in Lily's stomach. Why does she suddenly feel like BFF and Sandy going missing isn't a coincidence?

No. He is her friend. He wouldn't hurt Sandy.

But as she pushes deeper into the dark trees, a tiny voice whispers in the back of her mind, asking her: *Does she really know him at all?*

CHAPTER 10

There's something refreshing about sharing a meal with someone new. It had been a while since the Finches has welcomed someone into their home for the first time and Otto was enjoying every moment of it. Especially the look on his mother's face.

In Berlin, everything was as it always was. The same people. They have the same stories. The same gossip.

But there was something about Clementine Miller that brought a new light into the Finch house. Maybe it was her stories about serving as an undercover agent in Australia or her time working in the Pentagon—the stories she shared with Bernice and Otto were as if they were taken from a page of the James Patterson novels that Bernice read religiously.

Wine flowed.

And when the wine stopped, whiskey flowed after.

"I really can't thank you enough for inviting me," Agent Miller says as she takes a sip of her whiskey. It is one of Bernice's famous old fashioneds that includes just an extra dash of that thick cherry syrup from the Luxardo maraschino cherries to add a sweet finish to the punch of the whiskey.

"It's really our pleasure," Otto says. "Thank you for coming and thank you for everything that you're doing to find Sandy. Truly, our community is so grateful."

Clementine nods and pushes her braids over her shoulder as she looks down at the whiskey glass in front of her. She takes a deep breath, another sip, and looks as if she's having a hard time finding the right words to say.

She swallows hard. "Now that we've had a few drinks and we're all acquainted … can I ask you something that may seem a bit strange?"

Otto leans in and his heart flutters. "Yes—anything. Ask away."

"Chief Lavoie seems to think that Johnny and Kyle are on the come down from some very hard drugs. I'm no expert on New Hampshire but I know that there has been a severe drug epidemic in the past few years—especially in the North Country," Agent Miller explains. "But something doesn't feel right to me. It just feels off—I."

"Agent Miller, if I may," interjects Otto.

"Call me Clementine," she says as she lets out a small smile.

"Clementine, I know this is going to sound crazy. But I believe Johnny and Kyle. I believe them wholeheartedly. About the tunnels in the woods—I just know that they are telling the truth. They are innocent."

"How would you explain the blood on their shirts that's not their own?" Clementine challenges.

"Is it Sandy's?"

Clementine shakes her head as she smiles. Otto can tell by the way that her big brown eyes have lit up that she's enjoying their playful sparring.

"It's not Sandy's—but it's not Kyle or Johnny's either. We know that they got into some trouble … we just don't know what."

Otto takes a sip of whiskey and pushes his glasses up against his nose. "How do we know that they aren't victims? They're still kids, Clementine. For all we know—they could be victims of whoever is out there doing this just like Sandy. I believe them. And I believe that there are tunnels in the forest, whether Chief Lavoie wants to investigate them or not!"

"You really want to believe these boys," Clementine says as she lets out a low laugh. "You're going to stake your credibility on a bunch of teenagers?"

Otto nods so quickly that his glasses almost fall off his face. He's drunk, sure, but as always he is zealous in his beliefs. "With certainty."

Clementine lets out a small scoff.

"In my son's defense," Bernice says, "Otto has been through a lot and he has seen a lot that has really shaped his view of the world—"

"Mom, don't start," Otto says as a frown erupts on his face.

"What do you mean?" Clementine asks.

"My son, well. He um—"

"Mom. Stop."

Clementine looks down at her hands as she flashes her bright white teeth. "Come on, Otto. I'm not going to tell anyone. I promise."

Otto takes a long pull of his whiskey, the ice clinking against the glass. He glances at his mother, then back to Clementine.

"I was a freshman at Robin State College in '98," he begins slowly. "It was supposed to be like any other small New England town."

He pauses, his fingers tightening around the glass.

"Halloween that year … everything went wrong. They called it the Pumpkin Fest Riot, but that doesn't begin to describe what happened."

Otto removes his glasses, pinching the bridge of his nose. When he puts them back on, his eyes look distant, focused on memories rather than the present.

"It started with a student dying—one of the baseball players. Then another student was blamed for it. But that was just the beginning."

He takes another sip of whiskey, steeling himself.

"People started acting strangely. Suddenly turning violent for no reason. There was a girl in my history class—Jenny—who was always so quiet. One day she just ... snapped. Started screaming in the middle of class, tore books off shelves, emptied other students' backpacks. Her eyes were different, wild. And she wasn't the only one. It was like something was spreading through the town, making everyone lose control."

Bernice reaches across the table and squeezes her son's hand.

"I had a friend back then"—Otto's voice catches—"she believed there was something causing it all. Something in the town. The way Kyle and Johnny described being drawn into those woods ... it reminded me of how she described people acting in Robin."

"I remember hearing about this," Clementine says quietly. "It was on the news, wasn't it?"

Otto's laugh is hollow. "Some of it—*but not what really happened*. The *official* version. But I was there. I saw the things people did to each other. I watched a professor destroy her own classroom and bash her head into the wall until she died. I saw students who'd been friends for years trying to kill each other."

He leans forward, his voice dropping. "There was a professor there, a historian who specialized in ... unusual events. Dr. Brighton. She believed something was influencing people. Making them act on their worst impulses."

"Otto," Bernice warns softly.

"No, it's OK." He waves her off. "Most people in town blamed her, actually. Called her a witch; said she was causing it all. But she was the only one trying to stop it."

Clementine studies him carefully. "And what do you think caused it?"

Otto hesitates. "I'd rather not say, but it was evil. The violence spread through town like a disease. By Halloween night, it was complete chaos. The streets filled with blood. Fires everywhere. People turning on each other like animals."

He sets his glass down, his hand trembling slightly. "They banned Halloween in Robin afterward. No costumes, no jack-o'-lanterns, nothing that could 'incite' another incident. As if holiday decorations were what made people tear each other apart."

"You think something similar is happening here in Berlin?" Clementine asks.

Otto meets her gaze directly. "I think when teenage boys with perfect records suddenly find themselves covered in blood in the woods with no memory of how they got there, we shouldn't be so quick to blame drugs. I think when they talk about tunnels appearing where no tunnels should be, we should listen."

The silence that follows is heavy with unspoken thoughts.

"What happened to that professor? Dr. Brighton?" Clementine finally asks.

Otto's expression clouds. "Not sure. She left town right after. I tried calling her once, years later, but … she wasn't the same. It was like she wanted to forget."

He straightens in his chair. "So when I say I believe Kyle and Johnny, that's why. Because I've seen what happens when people dismiss the inexplicable as hysteria or drug use. People die."

Clementine sets down her glass. "I understand having experiences that don't fit neatly into reports." She leans forward. "If these tunnels exist, Otto, then we need to find them. Now."

"You believe me?" Otto asks, surprise evident in his voice.

"I believe you experienced something traumatic in Robin," she says carefully. "And I believe you're seeing parallels that concern you deeply. That's enough for me to take your theory seriously."

Otto nods, relief washing over his features. "Thank you. That's more than most people would give me."

"Well," she says with a small smile, "I'm not most people."

CHAPTER 11

"BFF, are you there?" Lily calls as she ventures deeper into the forest. Her small hand grips the flashlight tightly, its beam carving a semicircle of brightness against the darkness ahead. The yellow glow reaches only a few feet in front of her before surrendering to the shadows, making the towering trees around her seem even more daunting in the night.

Lily listens as her voice echoes throughout the forest. If only BFF would appear with his soft and kind voice and tell her that everything is going to be OK. She would feel so much better.

Lily looks over her shoulder at her home glowing behind her. When she narrows her eyes, she can see her grandmother and her father sitting at the dining room table with Agent Miller. They talk spiritedly, throwing their hands in the air, smiling and laughing like nothing has happened. Like Sandy never disappeared.

As Lily watches her father lets out a long belly laugh, it's then that she determines that she is all alone in this. Sandy's rescue is on her shoulders and hers alone.

She takes a deep breath and turns back toward the forest and decides to follow the path that heads up to the summit of Mount Jericho. It's about a three-hour hike to the top of the mountain—Lily and her dad have hiked the same path dozens of times. Never at night, but with her trusty flashlight, she believes she will be OK.

Listening closely to the sound of the woods at night, she walks further down the path. She doesn't hear much—just the sound of twigs crunching under her feet and the coo of a few owls. And crickets—the spring crickets are alive and well, clicking as she walks.

Until Lily hears something different.

Something unusual.

The sounds of the twigs cracking aren't only coming from under her feet now. They are coming from behind her.

She turns quickly and looks back, shining the light down the path she just came from.

There's nothing there.

It's just a forest, she tells herself. *Nothing more, nothing less.*

Continuing on the path, she knows if she can just find the entrance to the tunnel, then she will find Sandy. Maybe she will be there waiting? Lily could just take her hand and lead her back to the house like nothing ever happened.

She can't help but imagine her father's face if she were to bring home Sandy. Of course, he'd be mad at first for sneaking out. But Lily would be the hero of the whole town if she finds Sandy! One time Lily saw a segment on WMUR where a little boy just about her age saved an old man from a burning house. They called him a "hometown hero."

Imagine that.

Not only could Lily save her best friend in the whole wide world—she could be a hometown hero. Maybe Berlin would even have a parade in her honor?

As Lily walks she lets her mind wander. She almost forgets that she's walking alone in the dangerous woods at night when a familiar voice breaks through the air.

"Lily, is that you?" says a soft male voice from the bushes.

Lily's heart flutters and she pauses in her tracks. "BFF? Is that you?!"

Bushes rustle in the thicket to the left of her and Lily aims her flashlight beam toward the sound. The light catches only leaves and branches swaying gently, as if someone—or something—has just passed through.

"I've missed you, Lily," the voice says, warm and gentle like always. "You haven't visited me in a while. I've been lonely."

Lily's shoulders relax at the familiar tone. "I tried to! I came twice but you weren't there. I called and called."

"I'm sorry about that," BFF says, his voice moving slightly as if circling around her, always staying just outside her flashlight beam. "I've been … busy. Tell me, what brings you into the forest so late? Your father will be worried."

"It's Sandy," Lily says, her voice breaking. "She's gone. She disappeared during the Easter egg hunt and nobody can find her."

A long pause follows. The crickets seem to quiet. Lily can hear BFF shift with unease as twigs crack underneath him. He sounds so … big. Lily never noticed that before.

"That's terrible," BFF finally says, his voice softer now. "Poor Sandy. She was your real best friend, wasn't she?"

"I think she's in the tunnels," Lily continues ignoring his question. She turns in circles, trying to catch a glimpse of her friend. Something feels off to her. "The ones under the forest. I heard my dad talking about them. Do you know about any tunnels, BFF?"

Another pause. "Perhaps. Why are you looking for her alone, Lily? Why not let the grown-ups handle this?"

"Because they're not doing anything!" Lily stomps her foot in frustration. "They just sit around and talk while Sandy is out here somewhere. I have to find her. She's my best friend."

"Best friend," BFF repeats, his voice taking on a strange edge that Lily hasn't heard before. His voice sounds grainy— even desperate. "Yes, friendship is very important, isn't it?"

Lily nods vigorously. "That's why I need your help. You know the forest better than anyone."

"I do. That's why I'm your best forest friend," BFF says, and there's something different in his voice now—something that makes Lily's skin prickle. "I know everything that happens here."

Lily swallows hard. "Does that mean … do you know what happened to Sandy?"

"Perhaps," BFF says again, his voice suddenly closer. "But first, tell me, Lily. Has anything unusual happened to you lately? Anything … frightening?"

Lily thinks of the past few days, of her father's worried face, of the FBI agent asking questions, of the empty desk next to hers at school.

"Something scary happened a few days ago," she admits. "When I was walking to the bus stop, there was something in the bushes. It called my name, but it didn't sound like you. It sounded … wrong. It sounded evil and had these big yellow eyes. If I could be honest, I was hoping you would save me. That you wouldn't let whatever that thing is hurt me. I think that's what took Sandy!"

The forest goes completely silent.

"And what did you do?" BFF asks, his voice suddenly lower, rougher.

"I got scared and ran away," Lily says. "I told my dad about it."

The silence that follows makes Lily's heart pound harder.

"You ... told your father?" BFF's voice has changed entirely now—deeper, almost growling. "About something in the bushes calling your name?"

"Y-yes," Lily stammers, backing up a step. "I was scared."

A harsh, barking sound that might be a growl makes Lily jump. "You broke the rule, Lily."

"What?"

"The rule!" BFF snarls, his voice no longer staying in one place but seeming to come from everywhere at once. "Never tell your father about me! That was the rule!"

Lily's hand trembles, the flashlight beam dancing across the trees. "I didn't tell him about you," she protests. "I just said something called my name—"

"LIAR!" The voice booms so loudly that birds scatter from nearby trees. "You promised! I was going to help you. I was going to bring you to Sandy."

"You know where she is?" Lily gasps, momentarily forgetting her fear. "Please, BFF, please tell me!"

"I was going to bring you to Sandy," BFF continues as if she hadn't spoken, his voice pitched between fury and something that sounds almost like hurt. "But you broke the rule!"

CHAPTER 12

66 **I** think tomorrow you and I should go on our own search, to find the tunnels," Clementine says. "Screw Chief Lavoie. We don't need him. I just need someone who understands the area well and who isn't afraid of getting their hands dirty."

Otto smiles eagerly. "That's me. I would be happy to help you—we can do this together."

Bernice rocks back in her chair and furrows her brow. "I don't like this idea. I don't like it at all. The two of you going out into the woods by yourselves when you know something strange is going on. It's not safe. You need more numbers."

"Chief Lavoie isn't going to give us shit, Ma, you know that."

Clementine nods. "Otto is right—we can bring guns. We can protect ourselves; it will be fine."

Otto feels his mother look at him with the fury of a thousand souls. "And what are you going to do if you find these tunnels, eh? Go into them? Risk your lives? Risk Lily *losing another parent?*"

His mother's words hit him in the gut.

"If we find the tunnels we won't go down them, right, Clementine?" Otto asks eagerly. "We can just get the coordinates and we can come back to get help."

"Exactly," Clementine says. She opens her mouth to speak again, but she's interrupted by the sound of something coming from the woods. A scream?

The table rises and looks out the window toward the forest below Jericho Mountain. The dogs rise from their spots on the floor with their ears perked up as they start barking.

"Shush! Shush!" Bernice yells, urging the dogs to calm down.

Another scream comes from the forest; this one is even louder. The dogs begin barking in a fit.

"We should go," Clementine says. "Will you be my backup?"

Otto nods. "Do you have a gun—or something?"

Clementine lifts up her white blouse to reveal a holstered gun against her stomach.

"Excellent. I have one in the garage. Mom—can you stay here and look after Lily?" Otto says as he walks toward his mother.

Bernice nods and looks up at her son and puts both of her hands on his cheeks. "Please be safe. Please. And take Tiny with you. He will protect you."

• • • • • • • • ● • • • • • • • • •

Clementine and Otto step out into the cold spring night as they hear the screaming turn into loud, uncontrollable sobbing. Otto holds Tiny by the leather leash as they jog through the backyard and into the forest.

"Whatever you do," Clementine says as they pause at the threshold before crossing into the forest, "do not—and I mean do not—do anything crazy."

"What do you mean—do anything crazy?" Otto says with a light laugh. "I am gun safety certified, I will have you know."

Clementine rolls her eyes and pulls her braids back into a bun on her head. "OK. Just … let me take the lead, please."

Otto nods but before he can open his mouth to speak, the phone rings. He pulls the iPhone out of his pocket—it's his mother.

"Hurry, we have to go! Someone is hurt," Clementine says.

"One sec," Otto says as he answers the phone. "Mom—what's up? We are about to head into the forest."

A deep sob carries through the phone as Bernice has a hard time catching her breath. "Otto!" Bernice cries with heavy, hearty sobs. "Lily isn't in her bed."

Otto's stomach drops and his chest feels heavy. "What do you mean, Lily isn't in her bed?" he yells.

"She's gone! I looked everywhere!" Bernice cries. "Baby, I think she's in the forest! I think she's in trouble!"

CHAPTER 13

"You broke the rules, Lily!" BFF growls from inside the bushes. It's in that moment that Lily watches as her friend transforms from a light and happy companion to something darker and much more sinister. Two big yellow eyes the size of her fists light up from inside the bushes. They blink at her, warning her. The big circles pulse and glow and Lily can almost make out some parts of his figure.

Is he a person?

An animal?

Lily can't tell what he is—but she can tell that BFF is very, very big.

She backs away, her eyes wide with fear. "I'm sorry! I didn't mean to—"

"Friends keep secrets, Lily," BFF says, his voice suddenly calm again, which is somehow more frightening than his anger. "Even your stupid little friend Sandy understood that. Sandy *was* a good friend."

"Was?" Lily's voice breaks on the word. "Give me back my friend! Give me back Sandy, you evil monster!"

Something moves in her peripheral vision—something tall, something with long, pointed ears silhouetted against the darkness. But when she swings her flashlight toward it, there's nothing there.

"Tell me where she is!" Lily demands, trying to sound brave despite the tears streaming down her face. "Tell me where the tunnels are before I have my dad come and get you! He's going to find you, you know. He's going to find Sandy and you're going to be in a lot of trouble for a very long time."

"Go home, Lily," BFF growls.

Lily crosses her arms and stomps her feet on the ground. Sure she's scared, terrified even, but she's not going anywhere until she finds Sandy.

"I'm not leaving without her!" Lily screams in a fit of rage. She closes her eyes and clenches her fists and begins screaming so loud that she can't even hear BFF anymore. "I WANT SANDY. I WANT SANDY!" It's the first time she's yelled like this since she had a breakdown about a year ago. It was at Christmas and it was the first time that Lily realized in her young life that she would never have her mother and father back. She loved her adopted father of course, but when Lily first truly realized that the world took away her mom and dad, she couldn't control herself. She went into a fit of rage and cried for hours stomping in a fury. It wasn't fair. It wasn't OK. How could the world do this to little Lily Lemon?

To Lily, it feels like her world is ending.

The idea that BFF had something to do with Sandy's disappearance and now he won't tell her! Why? Why was this happening to poor little Lily? What did she ever do to this cruel world?

As Lily clenched her fists screaming, she felt something grab her arm tightly. Long, furry fingers that grip her so tight she worries that her wrist is about to snap. The grip is wrong in every possible way. It's not a human hand—the fingers are too long, too numerous. They're covered in coarse, matted fur that feels slick and oily against her skin. And they're strong, so impossibly strong that Lily feels the delicate bones in her wrist grinding together, threatening to snap.

When Lily opens her eyes and looks up at the creature that grabbed her so tightly—she screams even louder. Little Lily screams so loud that it disturbs everything in the forest.

And the creature—the thing that was never her friend— pulls her closer, its humid breath hot against her face as it whispers:

"Sandy screamed too, Lily. Right before she followed me home."

CHAPTER 14

When Otto learned that Lily's parents had died, it was like a piece of him had been carved out, thrown on the ground, and stepped on until his flesh was pulverized into a million pieces.

When Bernice told him that Lily wasn't at home sleeping in her bed like she should be, he felt that pain all over again except worse. He wanted to throw up. Pass out. His breath escaped him.

In that moment he wants badly to be that man he'd always wanted to be. Fight. Not flight. But Otto can't breathe. It's like someone has sucked every last breath of air out of his body.

Otto drops his phone onto the ground of the forest as Clementine stares back at him with her big brown eyes.

"What happened?" Clementine says.

Otto can't even get the words out of his mouth, but by his incoherent stuttering—she already knows. Clementine doesn't even think to bring Otto along with her. She snatches Tiny's soft leather leash out of Otto's hand and takes off down the path into the woods—sprinting as if Lily were her own daughter.

As tears well in his eyes, Otto tries to collect himself. He picks his phone up off the ground and takes off, running as fast as he can, trying to keep up with Clementine's athleticism.

His lungs burn as he runs stride after stride, pushing his way further into the dark woods. As he runs, his thoughts run through his brain like a washing machine tossing and turning and tumbling.

Will Lily disappear like Sandy?

Is she hurt?

Is she ... dead?

Otto pushes through the forest. He hasn't sprinted like this since the one time he tried junior varsity track at Berlin High School. Clementine is getting farther ahead of him and deeper into the woods. If he loses her, will whatever is haunting these woods take Otto too?

What if Otto has to fight?

What if Otto has to kill something?

Or someone?

As he runs he reminds himself that he will do anything and everything to save Lily. No matter what.

A thought races into Otto's mind as he runs. A memory — or a delusion—he's spent decades trying to bury.

Robin State College, Halloween 1998.

Otto was standing in Dr. Beatrix Brighton's study, fire poker clutched in his trembling hands as he faced a ravenous middle-aged woman ransacking the room. Her blond hair disheveled, her eyes bloodshot and wild.

"WHERE IS SHE!" the woman had screamed, spittle flying from her mouth. "I need to find that bitch and I need to kill her for what she has done to our community!"

Young Otto had warned her to step back, but she kept advancing—her eyes empty of reason, filled only with rage. The memory flashed forward—the woman pressing against the fire poker, the struggle on the floor, her hands crushing his windpipe trying to take his last breath. The desperate panic as his vision began to darken.

Then the sickening feeling of the fire poker piercing her flesh. The spray of blood across his glasses. The horrifying gurgle as he pushed it deeper into her neck. The way her body had twitched before going still.

Otto stumbled in the dark forest, catching himself against a tree trunk. For years, his therapist had convinced him that the strange things he'd seen were hallucinations—his mind's way of processing trauma. That these inexplicable parts of his memory were fabrications to help him cope with the violence he'd experienced.

But the therapist was wrong. Otto killed someone. And he may have to kill again.

Would he have to kill again to save his daughter? The thought made his stomach lurch. He'd spent decades convincing himself he wasn't a killer—that what happened in Robin was self-defense in extraordinary circumstances.

Otto pushed himself away from the tree and resumed running. He needed Dr. Brighton. She was the only one who had understood what they faced in Robin. The only one who might know how to fight whatever had taken Sandy and was now threatening Lily.

But first, he had to find his daughter. And if something was threatening her, Otto knew with cold certainty that he would do exactly what he had done twenty-seven years ago.

The fire poker. The blood. Life draining from the woman's eyes.

This time, he wouldn't spend decades trying to convince himself it wasn't real.

CHAPTER 15

Clementine Miller has seen some pretty scary shit in her time as an FBI agent. She's uncovered pedophile rings, sex trafficking, murderers, serial killers, gangs, drug rings—she's just about seen it all.

But nothing prepares her for this.

As she runs through the forest, the screams are getting closer and closer, as Tiny's long and lanky gait pulls her deeper into the darkness. She stops immediately when she sees it.

The thing that towers in the clearing isn't a rabbit—it's a mockery of one. It's a blasphemous corruption of nature that exists somewhere between a human, an animal, a cryptid, and blasphemy. It's an abomination. The creature stands nearly eight feet tall, its once-white fur matted with blood and viscous black streaks that glisten wet in the moonlight. Rust-colored smears are baked into its filthy pelt, and something pink is mashed in its fur that can only be flesh.

Its proportions are wrong. The limbs are too large; the joints bend in directions that anatomy doesn't allow. What should be harmless paws have stretched into grotesque hands with long meaty fingers—each digit fancied with a long yellow talon that drips with fresh blood.

The head is the worst part. The skull seems to have been stretched and distorted, with a jaw that hinges open far wider than any mammal should be capable of—revealing not the flat teeth of an herbivore but row upon serrated row receding into a throat that is impossibly dark and deep. Above that gaping mouth, its nose continuously twitches and writhes as if smelling fear itself, while those iconic rabbit ears are shredded and torn, chunks missing as though gnawed away.

But the eyes—the eyes—are what make Clementine's knees nearly buckle. Massive yellow bulging orbs that glow a sickly jaundiced yellow, with pupils that contract into vertical slits when they fix on her. As Clementine stares, unable to look away, she can feel those eyes penetrating her mind with sadistic delight.

It holds Lily by the arm with one grotesquely elongated hand, the child's legs dangling uselessly three feet off the ground.

Tiny lets out a whimper beside her—a sound Clementine never imagined such a massive dog could make —and she realizes that even this predator bred for hunting recognizes something fundamentally wrong with the creature before them.

The creature tilts its head at an impossible angle, nearly 180 degrees, and its mouth stretches into what might be a smile but looks more like a lesion tearing open across its face.

Tiny lets out a loud bark that causes the rabbit to jump. The creature lets go of Lily, sending her falling to the ground with a loud thud.

Clementine pulls out her gun and aims it at the abomination. "Don't move! Or I'll shoot!" she yells. Is it a man? A rabbit? Clementine can't tell but she steadies her gun as she shakes in her boots.

Tiny barks and barks, growling at the creature as he lunges for the beast, wanting to protect his little friend Lily.

Clementine looks down at Tiny. Should she let him go? Let him chase the beast into the woods further?

The rabbit ignores Clementine's warning and steps away from Lily and toward the thicket.

By the look in the creature's twisted eyes, she can tell that he can hear every word that she's saying.

"FBI. Don't move another inch or I will blow your brains out," Clementine yells.

The creature smiles a crooked smile and takes a step toward Clementine.

She fires her gun.

He takes another step.

Another bullet.

It does no good.

Another bullet to the brain.

Another step toward her with its massive rabbit feet.

His voice is sinister and sour like nails on a chalkboard. "I recommend you stop."

Clementine shivers when she hears his voice.

"I suggest you leave me alone. Don't tell anyone about this. Or more children will suffer, do you hear me?" the rabbit growls. The creature's yellow eyes twinkle with malevolent glee. "When you go to sleep tonight," it continues, voice dropping to a conspiratorial whisper, "just know I will be waiting in the forest. Waiting for you and your little mayor to fuck up. To tell someone about me. To try and come into the forest to *get me*. And when that happens, I will make sure that every last child in this shitty town ends up like Sandy."

Footsteps echo from behind Clementine as Otto catches up to her. He stumbles in a stupor, looking at the great depraved creature.

"Berlin is mine," the rabbit growls. "Run now. Take the child. But remember … I'll be waiting for you."

With that, the creature recedes into the thicket, its eyes the last thing to disappear—two gleaming points of yellow that linger unnaturally in the darkness long after the rest of it has gone.

CHAPTER 16

Otto sits in his car driving as fast as he can down 93 South, weaving in and out of the cars with his foot pressed hard on the gas. He's never driven this fast before. Otto is usually a pretty careful man, but he's on a mission. A mission for answers.

Otto didn't sleep the night before.

It was impossible.

After the creature escaped into the woods, Otto ran to Lily, picking up her little body in his arms and holding her tightly as she began to cry uncontrollably.

"He hurt Sandy. He hurt Sandy," Lily cried as she clenched Otto's jacket so tightly as if it were going to disappear just like her friend.

Clementine and Otto walked back through the forest with their eyes alert. Peeled for any more unnatural creatures or movements, but deep down they knew that whatever the beast was had spared them for some reason.

"He told me not to tell anyone," Clementine said as her voice shook. They trudged back through the forest trail with only the moonlight leading their way back to the Finch house. "He told me not to tell anyone or he would take more children."

Otto had nothing to say to Clementine. What could he say? That the military should come into the forest with every possible weapon they had to gun whatever that thing was down? That Chief Lavoie and Agent Miller should call their respective agencies and go on a manhunt for that creature until it is shot and killed?

Otto wanted to say all of these things except deep down he knew that none of them were possible. He and Clementine would be forced to sit with this knowledge until they could find a solution.

No one would believe them.

Everyone would think they were crazy.

Clementine would lose her job.

Otto would lose his reputation.

And no one would ever find Sandy.

So Otto did what he had to do. He hopped in his car and began a long drive down to Boston in search of answers.

The last address of Dr. Beatrix Brighton that was ever published was one that was in Cambridge, Massachusetts. It was a small colonial New England house right outside of Boston nestled in a quiet little neighborhood.

When Otto pulls up outside of the regal little home he's not sure what to expect. Will she remember him? Is she even alive? Does she even live here anymore?

Everything they shared was so long ago.

So much pain.

So much suffering.

Otto parks his Jeep out front and steps onto the cobblestone streets of Cambridge.

Brighton's place hunches under ancient oaks like it's trying to hide. Rogue wildflowers spill everywhere through the lawn. The old colonial has seen too many New England freezes to stay white anymore—just a tired cream that looks gold when the sun hits right.

The stone path doesn't bother with straight lines. It snakes through what might've been a garden once before nature staged a coup. Herbs Otto recognizes from his mother's kitchen—lavender, sage, rosemary—fight for space with herbs and weeds he doesn't recognize.

The porch sags in the middle, weather-beaten and stubborn. Wind chimes—too many—clink and rattle overhead like bony fingers. Plants spill from ancient copper pots gone green with age. Every window has some piece of stained glass stuck in it—moons, stars, symbols that probably mean something to somebody. They throw colored light across warped floorboards that have stories to tell.

A fat brass owl scowls from the purple door—actual purple, not lavender or some other bullshit. Its metal eyes follow Otto as he climbs the steps. A crooked sign beside it warns: NO SOLICITORS.

Otto wipes his sweaty palm on his pants before grabbing the owl. He knocks three times and waits, heart hammering against his ribs.

A shuffle of movement erupts from inside the house and for a moment, Otto can't believe that this is happening. That he's really here. That his past is about to come flashing at him like a bullet train.

The door creaks open, and green eyes emerge with a skeptical look, gleaming in the darkness. And then—a blink of recognition.

The door widens quickly and there she stands—Dr. Beatrix Brighton, her once-rich chocolate hair now a crown of silver that catches the afternoon light like a halo. Deep laugh lines frame her bright green eyes, which still hold the life that Otto remembers. Her face brightens with recognition, transforming from cautious curiosity to unbridled joy as she takes him in.

"Otto," she breathes, her voice warm like honey but with a slight quaver of age. "My goodness, look at you." Without hesitation, she steps forward and wraps her arms around him in a fierce embrace that belies her shrinking frame. The scent of chamomile and old books envelops him as she pulls back, holding his shoulders at arm's length to study his face.

"It's been so long," she whispers. "You look amazing. I always knew I'd see you again." Something in her expression tells Otto that despite the decades between them, despite all the normalcy she's built around herself, she hasn't forgotten what happened at Robin. How could she? "Come in," she says, stepping aside and gesturing into the warmth of her home. "I put the kettle on the moment I felt someone coming."

CHAPTER 17

D r. Beatrix Brighton sits across the table from Otto hanging on his every word. He looks so good—so grown-up and professional. When Dr. Brighton knew him, he was just a young freshman—long and lanky, with a head too big for his body— physically and emotionally. Otto was at first a skeptic. He didn't want to believe in anything paranormal or anything unusual.

He was smart, practical. And a friend of "real" science.

At first he brushed off Dr. Brighton as a bit of a "kook." That was until he saw what he needed to see. He saw evil—so much evil—with his own eyes. Dr. Brighton still felt horrible about it all. He was so young and he went through so much—violence, trauma, and of course losing his best friend.

And now here he was sitting across from her, telling her about how his own daughter lost her best friend.

"I heard that you took in Lily," Dr. Brighton says with a soft smile. "That was so kind of you."

Otto smiles weakly. "Well. What's one supposed to do when your best friend dies? And Lily—Lily is a great girl. I love her so much. I just hate that she's going through this. I know what it feels like—to have your best friend ripped away from you in an instant."

Dr. Brighton nods and takes a deep breath.

"So, the girl disappeared?" Dr. Brighton says as she wraps her frail hands around her warm cup of tea. Her house is bright and warm and feels like something out of *The Hobbit*. Her home presents a disorienting contrast—warm and inviting at first glance, yet disturbing upon closer inspection. Beneath the low-beamed ceilings and beside the crackling hearth, oddities lie around every corner.

A glass-encased jackalope skeleton perches on the mantel, its antlered rabbit skull grinning at visitors while nearby, a collection of Victorian mourning hair jewelry dangles from a bronze tree sculpture. Shelves overflow with mismatched curiosities: preserved two-headed chicks floating in formaldehyde, antique medical instruments with seemingly strange purposes.

Despite these otherworldly elements, the space remains somehow welcoming—colorful quilts draped over armchairs, fresh-cut wildflowers in crystal vases, and the smell of herbs and freshly baked bread.

"Yes, she disappeared on Easter Sunday," Otto says as he swallows hard. "And Lily was so distraught—so broken that she decided to go into the woods on her own to find her."

Dr. Brighton nods and narrows her eyes. "And what did little Lily find in the woods?"

Otto laughs as if he can't even believe his reality. "I um—I saw it too. And so did the FBI agent helping with the case."

Dr. Brighton shifts with unease at the mention of law enforcement. "You need to be very, very careful," she says as she shakes her head. "You cannot trust anyone to have your best interests at heart except for yourself."

Otto nods. "I know, I know ... but I don't think she's going to tell anyone because it told us not to. It said that if we tell anyone—if we try to find it—it's going to take even more children."

"And what did it look like?" Dr. Brighton asks.

Otto laughs again and shakes his head. "This is going to sound crazy."

Dr. Brighton laughs. "I've seen a lot of crazy in my time, Otto."

"Yeah ... I know. You're an expert in this type of thing. I'm sorry. But I um ..." Otto was having a hard time putting it into words. Did last night even happen? Was it real? Or just a fever dream? "Well, Dr. Brighton, it uh—it looked ... it looked like a giant demented rabbit."

Dr. Brighton leans back in her chair and nods slowly as if she knows exactly what plagued Otto's little mountain town.

"And it talked to you?"

"Yes—it was very disturbing. It was like half man, half rabbit … except worse. And its voice—it was broken and cracked yet somehow a little … enticing," Otto says as he folds his arms across his chest. "And Lily … she told me he's been watching her for months. That they've been talking in the forest like they were friends. But he evolved … into something much more … evil."

Dr. Brighton nods and takes a sip of her tea. "Very well then."

"What do you think it is?" Otto said. "A lab experiment gone wrong? A demon? I just—"

Dr. Brighton reaches across the table and grabs Otto's shaking hand. "Take a deep breath. This is not the worst news," Dr. Brighton says. "It's pretty clear what you're dealing with."

Otto's eyes light up. "Really?"

"You're dealing with a Bunny Foo Foo."

Otto lets out another awkward laugh. "A Bunny Foo Foo? You can't be serious. A Bunny Foo Foo?"

"Do you know the fable?" Dr. Brighton asks. She's not smiling or laughing. In fact, a frown crosses her face to show that she's serious. "The fable—it comes from Quebec."

"Really?" Otto says as his eyes widen.

"Yes, do you know the song 'Alouette'? It's quite similar in terms of tune. The actual fable and the song of Bunny Foo Foo come from Quebec. *Little Bunny Foo Foo, hopping through the forest, scooping up the field mice and bopping them on the head,*" Dr. Brighton recites, her voice taking on an eerie singsong

101

quality that makes Otto's skin prickle. "*Down came the Good Fairy, and she said—*"

"'*Little Bunny Foo Foo, I don't want to see you scooping up the field mice and bopping them on the head,*'" Otto finishes automatically, the childhood rhyme rising quickly from his memory.

Dr. Brighton's eyes darken. "Yes. But, Otto, this isn't just a nursery rhyme. It's much ... darker than that."

She rises from her chair with surprising agility for her age and crosses to one of her many bookshelves. Her fingers dance over old spines before pulling out a leather-bound volume so old the title has worn away. When she opens it, the musty scent of age fills the room.

"The creature you described—it's very real. It's called a Foo—otherwise known as a Fool, though over time the name became sanitized in children's stories as 'Foo Foo.'" She turns the book toward Otto, revealing an illustration that sends ice through his veins—a towering, malformed rabbit-like creature with distended limbs and glowing eyes, just like what they'd seen in the forest.

"The Fool isn't something summoned—it's something created," Dr. Brighton continues, her finger tracing the text beside the illustration. "In French Canadian folklore, particularly in the remote villages of Saint-Narcisse-des-Érables, there are accounts of witches who would transform their own children into these creatures as punishment for terrible deeds. The nursery rhyme we know today was a warning to children. If you don't behave, the Good Fairy—the witch—will turn you into a Fool! In some nursery rhymes it's a goon, but it's the same."

Otto nods along watching Dr. Brighton thumb through the old pages with succinct wisdom.

"But the original spell was a mother's last desperate act to contain evil that had already taken root in her child. She would bind her transformed son to the forest, hoping nature would temper his darkness. And the witch would leave her misbehaving son—or daughter, though most were sons—to the forest."

Otto stares at the illustration, his throat dry. "But why Berlin? Why now?"

"Well, lore says that most of the witches who turned their children into Fools … they still fed them. Every night they would go out into the forest and bring the Fools raw meat. That's all they craved. Bloody beastial meat. But when the Fools aren't fed, that's when they start to become what you've described. They change and develop a new kind of hunger."

"For children?" Otto asks as his eyes widen.

Dr. Brighton shrugs. "I've never dealt with a Fool on my own, but my thinking is that the children are just easy targets. You see, the Fool is still a bit human. It has a consciousness just like you and me. It still has a human soul."

Otto nods. "Well then, how do we stop it? How do we stop the Fool?"

Dr. Brighton's expression turns grave. "A Fool can only be created by someone with knowledge of very specific French Canadian witchcraft traditions. Old traditions. If there's anyone French Canadian in your little town—" She pauses, watching understanding dawn on Otto's face.

"I mean half the town is French Canadian," Otto laughs.

"Well," Dr. Brighton says. "You've got a lot of work to do, Otto. Because in order to stop the Fool, you need to find who created it. And get them to reverse the spell."

Otto nods. "It sounds easy enough, once I find the right person, right?"

Dr. Brighton shrugs her shoulders. "While it may sound easy, Otto, think of why a mother would want to turn her son or daughter into something so sinister and vile? Usually it's because they've done the unthinkable."

Otto's mind races through the residents of Berlin. Who could possibly be behind this? Who has a son or daughter who has committed unspeakable acts? Who has such a deep connection to Quebec that they would even know this old fable?

"The tunnels the boys described," Otto says suddenly. "Could they be—"

"Yes," Dr. Brighton nods. "In the lore, the Fool creates passages between our world and a pocket dimension where time moves differently. Days here might be minutes there. If Sandy is in those tunnels …"

"She could still be alive," Otto finishes, hope surging through him.

"Possibly. But Otto, listen carefully"—Dr. Brighton leans forward, gripping his hand—"the Fool can be defeated, but not with bullets or conventional weapons. According to the lore, there are three ways to end its reign of terror."

She holds up one finger. "One, find the witch controlling it and break their power or get them to reverse the spell."

A second finger. "Two, follow the rules of the nursery rhyme—give the Foo three chances to reform before turning it into something else. You're not a witch, so that won't work for you."

The third finger rises. "Or, three, say the incantation backward."

Otto's mind reels with the implications. "What incantation?"

Dr. Brighton smiles. "I don't know. I'm not a witch … despite what some may think."

Otto nods. "OK but—how do I identify the witch?"

Dr. Brighton's eyes meet his. "Look for someone who may have lived in Northern Quebec, or has an ancestry they're particularly proud of. Someone with a child, one who is rather unruly."

Something clicks in Otto's mind—a detail he'd overlooked.

"There's one more thing," Dr. Brighton says, her voice dropping to a whisper. "The Fool feeds on the innocence of children. It doesn't just take them; it transforms them. The blood on those boys' shirts? It wasn't Sandy's because Sandy isn't dead. It was animal blood—the Fool's way of marking them. If a child has been marked by the Fool—he knows where they are at all times."

"Marking them?" Otto asks, dread building in his chest. Is Lily marked?

Otto's phone buzzes in his pocket. With trembling hands, he pulls it out to see a text from Chief Lavoie:

Otto, shit's hitting the fan here. Those boys started screaming about 'yellow eyes watching them' an hour ago. Complete psychotic break. Having them transferred to Lakes Region psych ward. Even Clementine's acting weird—keeps staring at the woods behind the station. Need you back ASAP. Might be late though—Ma's 80th tonight, can't miss it. Said she'd kill me, ha. Call when you can.

Otto looks up at Dr. Brighton, panic rising in his throat. "I have to go."

She grabs his arm, her grip surprisingly strong. "Otto, please be careful. It may seem silly—like a goofy old rabbit but it's not. It's something much darker."

"I know," Otto's says as he swallows hard. "That's what Lily called it, her BFF," he breathes. "Best Forest Friend."

Dr. Brighton's face drains of color. "Then it's already begun. The children are being called. You have to find the witch, Otto. Before the Fool collects them all."

As Otto rushes toward the door, Dr. Brighton calls after him. "Remember—find someone French Canadian! Someone with a child who has done the most unthinkable evil."

Otto freezes in the doorway, a single name suddenly crystallizing in his mind.

"Oh my God," he whispers. "It can't be …"

TO BE CONTINUED.

EV Dean brings haunting New England folklore to life from the shadows of Los Angeles. She is a Phillips Exeter alum whose horror fiction walks the knife-edge between reality and nightmare. Dean has cultivated a devoted following with her chilling Bunny Foo Foo series and the Darkest Hour novellas. **You can follow EV Dean on Instagram at @EVDean_ author and order discounted, signed, paperback copies at EVDeanBooks.com .**

ACKNOWLEDGEMENTS

Special thanks to Priscilla, for reading early drafts and offering thoughtful feedback—especially around the racial and cultural elements of this story. Your perspective helped make the world of this book more honest, careful, and grounded. I'm grateful for you always and forever.

Big thanks to Dan Hanks—always positive, always sharp, and always exactly the editor I need.

Made in United States
North Haven, CT
02 July 2025

70275079R00069